JACK: SECRET CIRCLES

ALSO BY F. PAUL WILSON

YOUNG REPAIRMAN JACK*

Jack: Secret Histories

REPAIRMAN JACK*

The Tomb
Legacies
Conspiracies
All the Rage
Hosts
The Haunted Air
Gateways
Crisscross
Infernal
Harbingers
Bloodline
By the Sword
Ground Zero

THE ADVERSARY CYCLE*

The Keep
The Tomb
The Touch
Reborn
Reprisal
Nightworld

OTHER NOVELS

Healer
Wheels Within Wheels
An Enemy of the State
*Black Wind**
Dydeetown World
The Tery
Sibs
The Select
Virgin
Implant
Deep as the Marrow
Mirage (with Matthew J. Costello)
Nightkill (with Steven Spruill)
Masque (with Matthew J. Costello)
The Christmas Thingy
Sims
The Fifth Harmonic
Midnight Mass

SHORT FICTION

Soft and Others
*The Barrens and Others**
*Aftershock & Others**

EDITOR

Freak Show
Diagnosis: Terminal

*See "The Secret History of the World" (page 285).

JACK: SECRET CIRCLES

F. PAUL WILSON

A TOM DOHERTY ASSOCIATES BOOK
NEW YORK

This is a work of fiction. All of the characters, organizations, and events portrayed in this novel are either products of the author's imagination or are used fictitiously.

JACK: SECRET CIRCLES

A Tor Teen Book
Published by Tom Doherty Associates, LLC
175 Fifth Avenue
New York, NY 10010

www.tor-forge.com

Library of Congress Cataloging-in-Publication Data

Wilson, F. Paul (Francis Paul)
Jack : secret circles / F. Paul Wilson. — 1st ed.
p. cm.
"A Tom Doherty Associates book."
ISBN 978-0-7653-1855-8
1. Repairman Jack (Fictitious character)—Fiction. 2. Missing children—Fiction. 3. Monsters—New Jersey—Pine Barrens—Fiction. 4. Folklore—New Jersey—Pine Barrens—Fiction. 5. New Jersey—Fiction. I. Title.
PS3573.I45695J33 2010
813'.54—dc22

2009040678

First Edition: February 2010

Printed in the United States of America

0 9 8 7 6 5 4 3 2 1

JACK: SECRET CIRCLES

Little Cody Bockman disappeared on a rainy morning.

1

Jack dodged puddles as he pedaled his BMX along Adams Street to the Connell house. Even though the sky was overcast now, the air felt dry. He hoped it would last. He was sick to death of rain. People were saying this could turn out to be the rainiest September on record and—

"Hey!" he shouted as he almost collided with a little kid scooting by on a red bike. "Cody!"

The kid braked and almost fell off his bike.

"Jack! Jack! I can do it!"

"What?"

"Look! No training wheels!"

Cody Bockman was five and lived two doors down from Jack. His long hair was a blond tangle and his blue eyes sparkled with excitement. Cute kid, but a little wild man. Jack liked him except when he attached himself and followed him around like a dog. Somehow he always chose times when Jack felt like being alone.

"That's cool, Code." Jack looked around. Not an adult in sight. "Your folks know you're out here?"

"No, but it's okay."

"Yeah? You mean, if I go back and ask your mom and

dad if it's all right for you to be cruising the streets, they'll say it's fine with them?"

Cody looked down. "Well . . ."

Jack put on a stern look. "You gonna go or am I gonna have to take you back?"

"I'm goin'!"

He turned his bike around and pedaled a wobbly path back toward Jefferson. Jack watched him a little, then continued on to the Connells'.

Weezy's brother Eddie had asked him over to play *Berzerk*, the new game his father had bought him for his Atari 5200. The game was simple and so fun when you could trick the robots into walking into walls or shooting each other, but so nerve-racking when that deadly smiley face came bouncing through.

But no video games today. He'd played enough during the rains. This morning he was going to drag Eddie off the couch and into the sunlight. No easy task, considering Eddie's weight and resistance to any activity that involved moving more than his thumbs.

As Jack glided past the unlidded garbage cans at the curb—Wednesday and Saturday were garbage days in Johnson—he noticed a couple of familiar items from Weezy's room in the nearer container. He stopped for a closer look and saw copies of *Fortean Times* and *Fate*. Weezy treasured those weird paranormal magazines. Why was she throwing them out?

Maybe she was in a cleaning mood. She had all sorts of moods lately. Spin the dial and see who appeared.

Or maybe she didn't know. Her parents were always on her case for not being like other fifteen-year-old girls. Had they simply gone in and started tossing stuff? That wasn't right.

He spotted a half-folded photo, an aerial shot of the Pinelands, the million acres of woods beyond the town's eastern edge. He recognized the scene: an excavation of the mound where just last month he and Weezy had found a corpse and a mysterious little pyramid.

The sight of it released a flood of memories . . . most of them bad. He'd blocked them out, but now they were back. The dead man was not simply dead, he'd been murdered—*ritually* murdered—and his discovery had triggered other deaths, all seemingly of natural causes, but all weirdly connected. Then Jack had learned the cause, and it hadn't been natural at all. But he couldn't talk about it because he had no proof and everyone—even Weezy—would think he was crazy.

And the pyramid . . . shiny, black, embossed with strange glyphs . . . Weezy had fallen in love with it, memorizing every detail of the symbols on its sides and the weird grid inside the box that had held it. It had turned out to be older that it seemed—much older than anything man-made should be.

Then it had disappeared.

And Weezy hadn't been quite the same since. Jack had felt the loss too—such a neat artifact—but not like Weezy. She'd taken it like the loss of her best friend. But more than that, she was convinced it had been stolen and was sure she knew the culprit . . . all without a shred of proof.

So he couldn't believe she'd throw away this photo.

He snagged it from the can and stuck it in his back pocket as he hopped up the front steps and knocked on the door.

"Door's open," he heard a man's voice call from inside.

As Jack stepped in, Mr. Connell poked his crew-cut head

around a corner and grinned. "Eddie said you'd be coming. He's in the family room."

"Is Weezy here?"

"Yeah. Hey, Weez!"

"What?" Her voice floated from upstairs.

"Jack's here!"

Weezy appeared at the top of the stairway in her customary black jeans and a black T-shirt. She had dark eyes and pale skin. She'd gone a little heavier than usual on the eyeliner today. She held a book in her right hand, her index finger poked between two pages. She'd been letting her dark hair grow and today she'd parted it in the middle and braided it into a pair of pigtails.

"Hey, Jack. Come on up."

"Going for the Wednesday Addams look?" he said as he took the steps two at a time.

"Well, it's the weekend and I'm full of woe."

He followed her into her room, christened the "Bat Cave" by her brother. With all the shades drawn, a dark purple bedspread, gargoyles peering down from her bookshelves, and a creepy Bauhaus poster on the wall, it lived up to the name.

"About anything in particular?"

"The usual—everything." She belly-flopped onto the bed and opened her book.

"What's so interesting?"

"Just got it from the library. All about pre-Sumerian civilizations. What's up?"

Jack pulled the photo from his pocket and held it up. "I found this in your garbage can."

She glanced up with a smile. "Are you Dumpster diving now?" Then her gaze fixed on the wrinkled photo. "Isn't that . . . ?"

"Yeah. Never thought you'd toss it out."

She was up in a flash grabbing it from him.

"I didn't." Her expression turned furious. "They have no right!"

As she started for her door Jack blocked her way. She had a wild look in her eyes. Jack had seen that look a few times before when she'd lost it, and she seemed ready to lose it now.

"Easy, Weezy. Could you maybe wait on this? You're going to put me smack-dab in the middle of the fight."

For a second he thought she might hit him. He didn't know what he'd do if she tried. He was relieved when the look faded.

"Because you found it?"

He nodded. He didn't want to become a player in the ongoing tug-of-war between Weezy and her parents—mostly her father—who wanted her to be what they called "a normal girl" and what she called "a bow head."

"You know," she said, her voice thickening as she stalked about her room, "if they're so unhappy with me, why don't they just send me off to boarding school or something so they don't have to look at me?"

Jack didn't like that idea one bit. Who would he hang with? He tried to lighten the moment by clutching his hands over his heart and giving her his best approximation of a lost-puppy look.

"But-but-but wouldn't you miss *meeee*?"

It didn't work. She was off to the races. She'd always been hard to stop once she got rolling, but almost impossible since the disappearance of the pyramid. She'd gotten a little scary lately.

"I'm going to be fifteen next week! I've got a brain, why don't they want me to use it? They have no right to throw out my stuff!" She stopped her pacing. "Maybe I should pull a Marcie Kurek! That'd show 'em!"

Marcie Kurek was a runaway who'd been a soph at the high school last year. She lived in Shamong. One night she said she was going out to visit a friend and never showed up. No one had seen her since.

Weezy turned and threw the photo on the floor.

Jack knew she tended to leave her stuff all over the house, a perfect invitation for her folks to dump the things they didn't approve of, especially anything that referred to what she called the Secret History of the World.

The Secret History was her passion—her conviction that accepted history was a collection of lies carefully constructed and arranged to hide what was really going on in the world, and conceal the hidden agenda and identities of those pulling the strings. Ancient secret societies manipulating events throughout the ages . . .

People—especially her family—tended to roll their eyes once she got started on it. Jack too, though not as quickly as he used to. He'd seen and heard things last month that he couldn't explain . . . he didn't know if they fit into Weezy's Secret History, didn't know if they fit anywhere, or if they were even real.

Weezy was convinced that the pyramid they'd found was connected to the Secret History. And maybe it was . . . this was a picture of the mound where they'd found the body and the artifact, or rather what was left after those strange government men had dug it up in the night.

He glanced at it now on the floor and was once again struck by the strange outline. As he looked he noticed something to the right of the mound . . .

He picked it up for a closer look . . . a dark object or structure in a small clearing. He'd never noticed it before. But then again, the photo had been in Weezy's possession all this time, so he'd never had much chance to study it.

"Hey, Weez. Where's your magnifying glass? Or did your folks throw that away too?"

"Not funny."

She plucked a magnifier with a two-inch lens from a shelf above her desk and handed it to him. Jack poised it over the area in question and felt a tingle of excitement across his neck as it grew larger and came into focus.

"Oh, man, you've got to see this." He passed the lens and photo to her, then tapped the spot. "Right there."

He watched her brow furrow as she moved the lens up and down and around.

"Hmmph. Never noticed." She glanced up. "Could be just a big rock."

"Yeah? Take another look. Count the sides."

He watched her eyes narrow to a squint as she complied, then widen. She wore an entirely different expression when she looked up this time.

"Six."

"Yeah. Just like our pyramid."

A light sparked in her eyes. "Actually it had seven if you count the base. But this is bigger. Much bigger." She frowned. "Too big for them to steal."

Jack knew who "them" were but didn't want her to get started on that now.

"You got that right. Want to take a look?"

"You kidding? Of course I—"

"There you are!"

Jack turned and saw Weezy's portly brother standing in the doorway, twisting a Rubik's Cube. He had short, sandy hair and a pudgy body, and his striped rugby shirt gave him a definite Pugsley look. Jack was tempted to remark on the *Addams Family* theme here in the Connell house, but held his tongue. Eddie wouldn't take kindly to the Pugsley comparison.

But if Cousin Itt showed up . . .

"Hey Eddie. I was just—"

"No *Berzerk* today, man," Eddie said, looking miffed. "My dad's booting me out of the house. Wants me to 'enjoy the outdoors.' Can you believe it?" He shook his head sadly. "Boracious."

Eddie was not a fan of the outdoors, unless it meant sitting in the shade with a copy of *Uncanny X-Men.*

Jack pointed to the Rubik's Cube that had become Eddie's latest obsession. "Hey, anytime you want me to straighten that out for you, let me know."

He gave a wry grin. "Yeah, right. Like you could."

Jack shrugged. "Just trying to help the helpless."

Eddie glanced at his sister stretched on the bed and his grin turned evil. "You too, cave girl. He wants us both out in the"—he grabbed his throat and made a strangled sound—"fresh air."

"We were just leaving," Jack said.

"Where to?"

"The Pines."

Eddie shook his head. "No way. Last time I was in there with you two we found a dead guy, and pretty soon a whole bunch of guys were dead."

Jack shrugged. "Look at it this way: How many times can

that happen? Chances of finding another dead guy are almost zilch."

"You guarantee that?"

"Let's go," was all Jack said.

Nothing was guaranteed in the Pines.

2

They finally convinced Eddie to come along. Jack was leading the way off Adams onto North Franklin when he spotted a familiar blond-haired kid on a bike.

"Hey, Cody!" Jack called. "I thought you were going back home!"

"I am! I am!"

"Did you stop off in Canada along the way?"

The kid laughed. "No!"

Jack pointed toward Jefferson Street. "Better get back before your folks find out and sell you to the circus."

He grinned as he pedaled away. "That'd be soooo cool!"

Jack watched him turn the corner onto Jefferson and disappear from view, then signaled Weezy and Eddie back into motion.

"You handled that like a pro," Weezy said as they rode.

"Yeah, well, I'm positive his parents don't know he's out here. My mother knows his folks and she says he wears them out. Never stops moving."

She slapped Eddie on the arm. "*That's* where all your energy went. Cody Bockman stole it."

"I'm gonna sue," Eddie said. "No, wait. If I get it back I'll have to run around all the time. Forget it!"

Jack said, "Check it out," as he pointed to a colorful poster on one of the telephone poles.

It announced the arrival of the Taber & Sons circus. The show parked itself near Johnson for a few days every fall. Not a real full-blown circus like Ringling Brothers, just some rides, a few animals, a tent show, and a midway. The local dates had been inked in.

"Hey, it opens tomorrow," Weezy said. "Maybe later we can go watch them set up."

Eddie grinned. "Count me out. Watching people work wears me out."

"Look!" Weezy cried as they approached Quaker Lake. "I've never seen it so high."

Neither had Jack. The lake was overflowing its banks and puddling near Quakerton Road. Mark Mulliner's canoes sat upside down at the water's edge. Jack doubted anyone had rented one in a while.

Mr. Rosen had been talking all week about how the ground was saturated and couldn't hold any more water. Whatever came down had to run off somewhere, and much of it was flowing into the lake.

"It's all the rain," Jack said.

Eddie said, "Your obvious-fu very strong."

Jack had to smile. Yeah, pretty dumb thing to say. In defense, he puffed up his chest.

"That's 'Supreme Master of the Obvious' to you."

The level was even higher than yesterday when he'd crossed the bridge on his way to Old Town. Water was pooled around some of the lakeside benches and willows.

A number of his lawn-cutting customers lived in Old Town, the original settlement that had spawned the sprawling, thousand-person metropolis of Johnson, New Jersey. But the succession of rainy days was interfering with his schedule. Yeah, he could cut wet grass, but it always wound up looking crummy, and then he'd have to come back for a fix-up.

He'd swung by after school yesterday to see if the lawns were dry enough to cut. They were, so he'd raced home to get his mower. But as soon as he wheeled it out of the garage, the skies opened up again.

No mow, no pay. And the longer the grass, the tougher the job, and the longer to get it done. A vicious cycle.

As the three of them pedaled across the bridge over the lake, Jack glanced at a boxy, two-story, stucco building known around town as "the Lodge." It belonged to the globe-spanning Ancient Septimus Fraternal Order. A very secretive bunch, tight-lipped about its activities and purposes and membership, and highly selective about who it accepted.

It had lodges all over the world. Why they'd put one here in Johnson, New Jersey, no one knew. Well, Weezy knew—or thought she did. She said the Lodge was here before the town, that members of the Order had settled here in prehistoric times. But that was part of her Secret History of the World, and the Septimus Order played a big role in it.

Membership was by invitation only, and this Lodge was rumored to include some of the state's most influential and powerful people.

Weezy glared at the building as they passed. "You want to find our pyramid, look in there."

Jack was ahead of Eddie but could hear an eye roll in his tone as he muttered, "Here we go."

"It's true," she said.

Against his better judgment, Jack said, "Things *do* get lost, Weez. It happens all the time."

"Things that are clues to the Secret History don't get lost, they get hidden away. The Order's job is to keep the Secret History secret. If we searched that place, we'd find it."

"Fat chance," Eddie said. "What are you gonna do, get invited in for milk and cookies?"

"I'll think of something. And you'll come with me, right, Jack?"

Jack glanced at the Lodge's barred windows and figured it was safe to agree—no way they'd ever see the inside of that place.

"If you're there, I'm there."

They passed the empty and supposedly haunted Klenke house that had been for sale ever since Jack could remember, and then the home of the town's supposed witch, Mrs. Clevenger. Jack had heard stories about the weird smells and noises in the Klenke place, but he'd never been in there himself, so he couldn't say if they were true or not. He had, however, come into contact with Mrs. Clevenger on a number of occasions since the summer, and though she was strange and never gave a straight answer, she wasn't a witch. Who believed in witches and hauntings anyway?

They approached the place where Quakerton Road ended and the Pine Barrens began. Jack recognized Gus Sooy's pickup parked by the lightning tree. A lot of folks said Gus's moonshine—known as applejack—was the best in the Pinelands. Jack also recognized the guy buying from him.

So did Eddie. "There's Weird Walt," he said from behind Jack. "Stocking up."

"Hey," Weezy called as she brought up the rear on her banana-seat Schwinn. "Don't call him that."

She and Walt had a strange bond, and she always took his side.

"It's gotta be eighty degrees out and he's wearing leather gloves and you're telling me he's not weird?"

Jack glanced over to where Walt was watching Gus Sooy fill a quart bottle with water-clear liquor from one of his big brown jugs. Hard to argue against him being weird. Folks said Walter Erskine hadn't been right since he'd returned from Vietnam. He said weird things and wore gloves day in and day out.

"He's a good guy," Jack said as they turned onto a firebreak trail and followed it into the Pines.

Weezy moved up beside him. "How would you know?"

"He comes into the store every now and then and we talk. He—"

A helicopter, heading southeast, did its *wup-wup-wup* thing overhead and Weezy stopped for a moment to stare with an anxious expression.

Jack understood her reaction. A few weeks ago, late one August night, government men—at least Jack assumed they were from the government—had used black helicopters to fly backhoes into the Pines and dig up the mound where he and Weezy had found the pyramid and the corpse. Who had told them about the mound? Who had sent them to tear it apart? These were questions he doubted he'd ever answer.

"It's not black," he said. "And it's not headed our way. Probably some high rollers headed for AC."

Gambling had been legal in Atlantic City for half a dozen years now and was enormously popular.

Weezy said nothing as she pulled ahead to lead the way. She always rode point when they were in the woods. Made sense. She knew this corner of the Pine Barrens backward, forward, up and down. She never got lost.

As they rode, the forty-foot scrub pines thickened on either side, stretching their gnarled, green-needled branches overhead as they lined the path like sentinels guarding their woodland domain. Jack checked the overcast sky through the needled canopy. This was the kind of day when people got lost in the Pines and were never seen again. But no worry about that with Weezy along.

Weezy led them along the dipping, deeply puddled trail onto Old Man Foster's land. Foster was something of a mystery. Nobody had ever seen him or seemed to know who he was, but he kept his land heavily posted with signs warning against fishing, hunting, trapping, and trespassing. Jack ignored them. He figured obeying the first three out of the four was good enough.

At least he wasn't trapping like a certain someone was doing around a spong they'd be passing along the way.

When they reached the spong they saw Mrs. Clevenger standing with an armload of sticks. She wore her usual long black dress and a black scarf around her neck—which made as much sense in this weather as Walt's gloves. Her three-legged dog sat to the side, watching their approach. The big, floppy-eared mutt had the thick body of a rottweiler but with lots of other breeds mixed in. Its right front leg was missing as if it had never been—not even a scar.

Weezy stopped and waved. "Hi, Mrs. Clevenger. Need any help?"

"No, dear. I'm doing fine."

Some Piney had been setting leg-hold traps around the spong—the local term for a wet low spot—trying to catch coons and possums and such when they came for a drink. Mrs. Clevenger had been coming out regularly and springing the traps with sticks. Jack wondered what the trapper would do if he ever caught the old lady at it. Whatever it was, he'd have to get past her nameless dog, and that wouldn't be easy.

Eventually they reached a burned-out area deep in the Pines. They knew the place well. Maybe too well. Here was where they'd dug up the little pyramid and the corpse.

After they'd leaned their bikes against some trees, Jack stood in the shade and pulled out their aerial photo of the area. Judging by the position of the midmorning sun, they'd been following the fire trail eastward. The mound lay to the right of the trail, which meant south. The strange-looking thing he'd spotted on the photo was to the right of the mound, which meant farther south.

He pointed to the burned-out area. "This way."

As they walked a weaving course around the blackened tree trunks, Jack saw green branchlets poking through the charred bark. Hard to kill these pines. Fires were common in the Barrens during the summer and fall, mostly the fault of campers and lightning. With all the recent rain, he doubted they'd see any fires at all this season.

"Think anything's left in there?" Jack said, pointing to the ruins of the mound as they passed.

Weezy shook her head. "Look at it. It's not even a mound anymore."

She had a point. The government men had left little more than a twisty-turny trench, now filled with stagnant water.

The pines thickened past the burned-out area, slowing their progress.

"This better be worth it," Eddie said.

Jack had known it was only a matter of time before he'd start complaining. He was kind of surprised he'd held off this long.

"Shouldn't be too much farther now. According to the photo, we should hit a clearing any . . ."

He stopped and stared as he spotted an open area dead ahead.

". . . minute."

The clearing hadn't surprised him, but what stood in its center stopped him cold.

Weezy pushed past him, then stopped, saying "Ohmy-god!" over and over.

Jack couldn't speak. The Pines were full of secrets and surprises, but this . . . this was over the top. Way over.

3

"What *is* it?" Eddie said from behind.

"Some sort of . . . pyramid."

At maybe fifteen feet tall, it had nothing height-wise on the ones in Egypt, but this was definitely a pyramid, and unlike any Jack had seen or heard of. He wondered if anyone alive today had ever laid eyes on it.

Weezy finally stopped saying, "Ohmygod!" and the three of them approached the pyramid. The closer they got, the odder it became.

As Jack neared he noticed it wasn't solid. Huge, elongated triangular stones stood in a circle, their bases buried in the sandy soil with their pointed ends jutting skyward and leaning toward each other.

"Look like Godzilla pizza slices," Eddie said.

A typical Eddie comment. If he wasn't thinking about video games, he was thinking about food. But his comment hit the mark: the structure did resemble half a dozen giant petrified pizza slices, crusts down and arranged in a circle.

A three-foot-high wall of headstonelike rectangular slabs ringed the whole thing.

They marched around it in silence. One of the triangular megaliths was broken halfway up, but the undamaged points of the remaining five met and leaned against each other at the pyramid's apex.

"Notice, Weez? Six sides . . . just like our little pyramid."

The gleaming black artifact they'd found in the mound

back there would have fit inside a softball. It too had six sides—seven if you counted the base.

Weezy nodded but said nothing. She seemed in a daze, incapable of speech or even taking her eyes off the pyramid. Jack thought he knew how she felt: She'd lost a little piece of the Secret History, but found something much bigger. He felt it too. The strangeness, the ancient, alien feel to the structure.

They came to a broken fence stone. Without a word, Weezy stepped over it and entered the circle. Jack followed but Eddie hung back.

Jack turned to look at him. "Coming?"

Eddie looked uncomfortable. "This whole place is majorly creepacious."

Jack agreed, but he put on a smile. "Don't worry. Weezy will protect you."

Eddie rolled his eyes and stepped over the broken slab. "I should know better by now to go anywhere with you guys. You find dead bodies, you get me locked up in a police car and chased by the cops, but do I learn? Nooooo."

"Look, Jack."

Weezy was standing by one of the leaning megaliths, rubbing her hand over the surface. Her expression was triumphant, beaming vindication. He imagined this was what Percival looked like when he glimpsed the Holy Grail.

"What have you got?" he said, approaching.

"Look familiar?"

With a trembling finger she traced a circle around a faint indentation in the weather-smoothed surface of the stone. Jack squinted until he could make out the full outline, then he gasped. Recognition was like a punch in the chest.

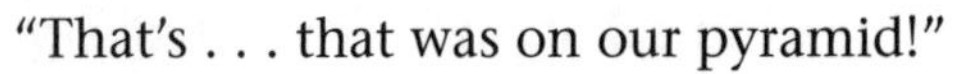

"That's . . . that was on our pyramid!"

She nodded and jumped to the next where she again ran her hands over the surface. She seemed about to explode.

"So was this one."

Then to the next stone.

Her voice shook. "This one too."

They were connected. No question.

"So . . ." he managed, swallowing hard as he stepped back for a longer look. "Is this based on our little pyramid, or was ours based on this?"

She shrugged. "Who can say? No way they're not connected. I mean, they're too much alike. But our pyramid wasn't made of stone."

Right. They'd given it to Professor Nakamura who'd had it analyzed at the University of Pennsylvania. No one there could say what it was made of, but it sure hadn't been stone. All they'd been able to say was that it was many thousands of years old—and then it had disappeared.

Jack stepped up to one of the megaliths and felt its surface. "Granite?"

Weezy moved up next to him. "That's what it feels like to me. Except . . ."

"Except what?"

"There's no granite in the Barrens, or anywhere near here."

Jack never understood where Weezy got all her information, but he'd learned to believe her. She wasn't a bull slinger.

Eddie joined them, saying, "So that means somebody cut these pizza slices somewhere else, drove them all the way out here, and made a teepee out of them. What for?"

Jack was thinking that "teepee" was a pretty good description when Weezy said, "'Drove'? I don't think so. Can't you see how old these are? I'll bet they were dragged here on rollers."

Jack looked at the stones and tried to imagine their weight, and the work it must have taken to carve each from a block of granite and then transport it here from wherever. He remembered Eddie's last question.

"But *why*?"

"And look," Eddie said. "It's not even put together right. They left spaces between the rocks."

"They've probably shifted over the ages," Weezy said.

Jack wasn't so sure about that. He'd noticed the spaces, but they seemed pretty uniform. Wouldn't shifting and settling over time have resulted in uneven gaps? These all looked to be an even ten or twelve inches apart at their bases, tapering as they went up. That couldn't have happened by chance.

He peered through one of the gaps. The empty space within was lit by strips of daylight streaming between the stones. Its floor lay about three feet below ground level under a couple of inches of rainwater. Jack could make out a layer of sandy soil beneath the surface. A stone column, maybe a foot in diameter and four feet high, stood in the exact center of the space.

Weezy and Eddie had moved up to gaps of their own on either side of him.

"It *is* a teepee!" Eddie cried. "Just like I said: a stone teepee!"

Weezy's voice dripped scorn. "A teepee is a place to live, so it needs a doorway—you know, one of those handy openings you use to get in and out? Plus, it's supposed to protect you from the weather. This flunks on both."

"All right, Miss Know-It-All, what is it then?"

Weezy hesitated, then, "I don't know. But maybe if I look at it from another angle . . ."

To Jack's surprise, she turned sideways, squeezed through the gap, and jumped down to the inner floor. She landed with a splash. He noticed she was wearing old sneakers. He looked down at his own battered Converse All-Stars. They'd been soaked before, no reason they couldn't get soaked again.

Jack squeezed through his gap—a tight fit but he made it—and eased himself to the floor to avoid splashing Weezy. Cool water filled his sneakers as he looked up and saw Eddie watching from outside. He made no move to join them. Jack was about to coax him in when he realized that even if Eddie wanted to join them, he couldn't. No way he'd fit through the narrow opening. Or worse, if he forced himself in, he might not be able to get out.

Jack turned in a slow circle, uncomfortable with the trapped feeling that stole over him. He saw a triangle of cloudy sky above the damaged megalith. The broken-off apex rested at an angle against its base.

What had happened? A weakness in the stone? A lightning strike? He'd never know.

"Look," Weezy said, pointing to the perimeter of the sunken area.

Jack saw how the sides sloped away at an angle, following the inner surfaces of the megaliths.

"How deep do you think the stones are buried?" she asked.

Jack shrugged. He had no idea, but the megaliths were even bigger than they appeared from the outside.

He heard splashing and turned to see Weezy making her way toward the short column in the center. Her speed increased until she all but leaped the last few feet.

"Jack! Look at this!"

When he joined her he found her running her hands over the top of the column.

"Look! It's the same shape, the exact same size!"

Jack immediately saw what she meant—a six-sided indentation in the top of the column, a perfect fit for their lost little pyramid. No doubt about it now—the two pyramids were connected.

"What do you think it did here?"

"I don't know but . . ." Anger washed across her features, leaving steely determination.

"But what?"

"Somehow, some way, I'm going to get our pyramid back and find out."

Jack shared her desire but couldn't see any way to make that happen, so he looked for a way to change the subject. He turned and pointed to the megaliths.

"Why go to all the trouble to drag these things here and set them up like this?"

Weezy shook her head. "Stonehenge was set up as a sort of solar calendar. Maybe this is something like that. Maybe the sun shines through one of these cracks and—ohmygod!"

"What?"

"Our pyramid. I'll bet they placed it right here in the center so that at certain times of the year a shaft of sunlight hit it and . . ."

"And what?"

She looked at him with a lost expression. "I don't know. But I've *got* to know. And I *will* know."

But Jack was thinking about something else. He did a slow turn, taking in the placement of the megaliths, the spaces between, the way they were tilted inward, making them virtually impossible to climb . . .

He felt a little squeeze in his chest as it all came together.

"I don't know about sunbeams and that sort of stuff, but look around. Imagine you're a tiger or a lion . . . those openings are wide enough to toss food inside but too narrow for something big to squeeze through. I think this is some sort of cage."

4

After a moment of stunned silence, Weezy said, "You could be right, but . . . but we're talking a major, major project. Chiseling these huge stones somewhere and dragging them here, then somehow setting them upright with exactly the right spacing between them, all to cage a lion?"

Eddie's voice was hushed. "Who says it was a lion. Maybe it was the Jersey Devil."

A glance told Jack that Eddie wasn't kidding. He liked to bring up the Jersey Devil as the cause of whatever couldn't be explained in the Pines—and there was no shortage of the unexplained here—but usually he was at least half kidding. This time, however . . .

Supposedly, back in the 1700s, a certain Mrs. Leeds, on learning she was pregnant for the thirteenth time, cursed the baby, saying she'd rather bear the devil's child than another for her husband. Well, that child was born with the head of a horse, bat wings, cloven hooves, and a spiked tail.

At least that was one version. Jack didn't buy into the JD. Neither, of all people, did Weezy, who bought into just about everything else.

Weezy did believe that *something* strange lurked in the Barrens, and Jack couldn't disagree.

"Eddie," Weezy said in her must-I-explain? voice, "this was built *way* before the first Jersey Devil story. It's got to be thousands of years old."

"No way!"

"Why not? Stonehenge was started in something like three thousand B.C."

Eddie shook his head. "Nuh-uh. The only people around here back then were the Lenape Indians, and they didn't build this."

Jack smiled up at him. "Well, you did say it looks like a teepee."

Eddie drew an invisible "1" in the air. "Got me."

"Other people were here besides the Lenape," Weezy said.

Eddie frowned. "Like who?"

"The Ancient Septimus Fraternal Order."

"The Lodge? No way!"

"Why not? The first word in their name is 'Ancient.'"

"This is your Secret History of the World stuff that nobody believes in but you." Eddie waved his hands. "But I don't want to get into that. What I want to know is, if this was a cage, what was in it? And where are its bones?"

Weezy dug the toe of her sneaker into the sand under the water, kicking up milky clouds.

"Probably under here. Who knows how much sand and dirt have blown in through the centuries? That wall out there probably kept out a lot of it, but I bet this is a couple of feet deep. And I also bet somewhere below is a big hexagon of granite that served as the original floor."

As Jack watched the churned-up water, he noticed the reflection of a blotch of light. He glanced up at the opening atop the damaged megalith. He dropped his gaze to the cracked-off chunk of granite leaning against its base. He imagined an animal—a bear, a lion, or whatever—climbing upon the fallen piece and then leaping, scrabbling, clawing its way to the flat, broken surface atop the megalith. From there all it had to do was slide down the outer surface and run free.

"It escaped."

Eddie and Weezy stared at him.

"How do you know?" she said.

Jack pointed to the opening. "Through there."

Weezy looked up, then down at the fallen piece, then nodded. "I think you could be right."

"That still doesn't answer the big question: Who would go to all the trouble to cart these stones here and set them up to cage an animal?"

Jack could not resist. "What if it wasn't just any animal. What if it was . . ." He paused, then screamed the last words. *"The Jersey Devil!"*

Eddie and Weezy both jumped, then Weezy laughed. "You've been hanging around him too long. Weren't you listening? It can't . . ." But her smile faded as she said, "On the other hand . . ."

Eddie grinned. "Hah! Told you it was the JD."

"No, it wasn't. But maybe it *became* the Jersey Devil."

"What are you talking about?"

"Did you ever hear of cryptozoology?" She quickly waved a hand at Eddie. "Never mind. Look who I'm asking. It's the study of strange creatures that may or may not exist."

Jack had never heard of it, but had an idea what it was about.

"You mean like Sasquatch and the Loch Ness monster?"

She smiled and nodded. "And yeti and the kraken and a bunch of others. So, what if ancient folks—maybe early, early members of the Lodge—built this to house some weird creature? Or maybe two of them—male and female. Maybe they were sacred to them, and maybe the little pyramid sitting in the center here had some significance or some function."

"Like what?"

"I don't know—yet. But what if they escaped into the wild? And what if they had offspring and their offspring had offspring? Eventually the Pilgrims came and the colonies started, and one day someone sees one of these things. And then somebody else sees it. Pretty soon someone makes up the Jersey Devil story to explain it. The story starts circulating and eventually we have a Pinelands legend."

"But what . . . ?" Eddie paused and Jack saw him swallow. "What if one of those things is still around?"

Weezy grinned. "Wouldn't that be cool?"

"Hey, guys," Eddie said. "Let's get out of here."

"What for?" Jack said. "We just got here."

"Because I see footprints up here. Big ones."

5

Jack froze. He glanced at Weezy and saw her standing statue-still as well.

"Where?" he said. "You mean here? Nearby?"

Eddie looked around. "Right behind me. Didn't notice them before—I mean, who would with this thing sitting in front of you—but they're here." He dropped to one knee and thrust his arm through the gap. "Here, Weezy. I'll help you up. See for yourself."

Jack blinked. Eddie offering to give his sister a hand . . . he must *really* want out of here.

Weezy looked a little surprised too, but took his hand. Her foot slipped as she tried to climb up. Jack instinctively raised a hand to give her butt a boost and instantly thought better of it. Not a good idea. Instead he wove his fingers and held out his interlocked hands for her to step in.

"Here."

The sole of her wet sneaker landed on his palms and he boosted her up. Once she was out he made a point of hoisting himself up and through the gap without help.

His feet squished in his sneakers as he checked out the sandy soil. He saw their own footprints, clean and crisp in the damp sand, but where—?

And then he spotted them—a line of indistinct, oblong depressions trailing along the perimeter of the pyramid.

"I thought you meant fresh tracks," he said. "These are old."

"Not that old. With all the rain we've been having, they wouldn't be there at all if they were old."

Jack had to admit he had a point.

"They're kind of big," Weezy said in a small voice.

Eddie pointed at the nearest. "'Kind of'? That's a foot long if it's an inch. Maybe longer. It could have been made before the last rain." He looked around. "Let's not kid ourselves, okay? There's something out here in the Barrens. We saw it that night when the government guys were digging up the mound."

Jack remembered the hulking shape silhouetted through the trees. Whoever it was had made Pepe le Pew smell like a rose.

"Oh, that. Probably just some big piney who hadn't had a bath since Christmas. All we saw was a shadow."

"A *big* shadow. I don't want it showing up here."

"It won't," he told him.

Eddie looked around again. "Yeah? People go missing in here every year. We all say they got lost and starved to death—"

Jack smiled. "You always say the Jersey Devil got them."

"I'm not kidding, Jack. What if they don't starve? What if something gets them and that's why they never make it back?"

Weezy looked at Jack. "Maybe we should go."

"Hey, wait. The Pinelands cover a million acres. Even if there is something out there, the chances of it crossing paths with us are pretty slim."

"I'm not so sure about that," Eddie said. "This cage or whatever may be special to it. Maybe it comes back here, like, regularly."

Jack had to admit they were getting to him. He looked

around and sniffed the air. Saw nothing, smelled nothing. Still . . .

"All right, all right. We'll head back."

They retreated through the burned-out area to their bikes, with Eddie, of all people, leading the way.

"Y'think we're the only ones who know about that pyramid thing?" he said once they were on their way back toward town.

Jack noticed he'd relaxed since putting some distance between himself and the pyramid.

Weezy nodded from the lead spot. "Good chance. Otherwise people would be yakking about it all over."

"Hard to believe no one's ever found it before us," Jack said.

Weezy slowed and let his bike pull even with hers.

"Maybe the Indians knew about it. And maybe some pineys do, but they keep to themselves. It's not like people are looking for it. And like you said: a million acres of woods. There are places in here no human has ever laid eyes on. Don't forget, that's on Old Man Foster's land. It's even less likely for hikers or campers to be wandering around posted property."

"Think Mister Foster knows about it?"

"I'd bet not. He doesn't seem to take much interest in his land. No one's ever seen him. For all we know, he's dead."

"Then who's posting all these no-trespassing signs?" Eddie said.

Jack and Weezy answered in unison. "The Jersey Devil!"

"Fine," Eddie grumbled. "Be like that."

Weezy said, "No big deal to hire someone to post signs."

Eddie looked at her. "Y'think we should tell anyone what we found?"

"Don't even think about it!" Weezy cried.

"Why not? Maybe some experts can come down and figure out what it really is."

"I'll tell you what they'll come down and do." She was talking through her teeth and Jack could sense the fury building in her. "They'll dismantle it and ship it off to the Smithsonian or something. You saw what they did to our mound. What makes you think they'll have any more respect for that pyramid?"

"'Our' mound?" Jack said with a smile, trying to cool her down. "When did it become ours?"

She gave him an annoyed look. "*I* know it's on Old Man Foster's land, and *you* know what I mean."

That triggered a thought. "Foster . . . they'll have to get his permission first."

Her voice rose. "Those guys who dug up our mound didn't have his permission! They just came in the middle of the night and did whatever they wanted to do, then left. They'll do the same with the pyramid!"

"Easy, Weezy." He seemed to be saying that a lot lately. "We'll keep our lips zipped."

She gave him a pointed look. "That means we don't tell *anyone*. Not even Mister Rosen, and *especially* not Professor Nakamura."

Jack figured Mr. Rosen could be trusted, but agreed about the professor. They'd lost the baby pyramid because of him.

"Mum's the word."

"Good." She looked at Eddie. "You with us, dear brother?"

Jack tried telepathy: *Agree with her.* Maybe it got through, or maybe Eddie knew better from experience.

"All the way, dear sister." He shrugged. "Besides, who'm I gonna tell anyway?"

"It's like a duty," she said. "The Barrens are special. They've kept secrets for ages. We can't go messing things up just because we got lucky. We—"

"Goddamn you little bastids!"

The shout came from off to their left and Jack was surprised to see they'd reached the spong already. The source of the cursing was a skinny man wearing an Agway gimme cap and bib-front overalls. He was hurrying their way, weaving among the traps Mrs. Clevenger had sprung. He snatched an upright stick from one of the traps and began waving it in the air.

He looked furious as he shouted, "I warned you 'bout messin' with my traps!"

They'd run into this piney before. He claimed he was Mr. Foster's son but Jack had a feeling Old Man Foster wasn't a piney.

"We didn't touch them!" Eddie called back, then spoke under his breath. "Least not this time."

"Hell you didn't! This is the second time now I find you here with all my traps sprung! I'm gonna teach you bastids a lesson you'll never forget!"

He broke into a run, whipping the stick back and forth ahead of him.

Eddie let out a wail and hit his pedals. His rear tire fishtailed and kicked up sand as he accelerated. Jack and Weezy were close behind. As they raced away, a fist-size rock sailed through the air, narrowly missing Weezy's head.

A blast of rage blazed through Jack. He felt his lips pulling back from his teeth in a snarl as he looked back at the piney.

The skinny man had stopped running and was screaming something incoherent as he waved the stick.

What if that rock had hit Weezy? What would he have done?

"Jack?"

Weezy's voice.

He looked and found her staring at him with a worried look.

"What?"

"You . . . you looked kind of scary just now."

"Didn't you see that rock? It just missed you."

"I know. But the important word is 'missed.' You looked like you wanted to kill him."

For a second there, Jack realized, that was exactly what he had wanted to do.

"Just don't like people throwing rocks at my friends."

She kept looking at him. "We *are* friends, aren't we."

"We are. Old friends."

"I like that."

The fading rage was replaced by a warm glow that hung on until they found the lost man.

6

Eddie had sped on ahead, racing back to town while Jack and Weezy took their time, talking. Or rather, Jack listening to her rattle on about the two pyramids and wonder how they fit into the Secret History. She glowed with excitement and vindication. She started talking about finding a way into the Lodge to retrieve their little pyramid. He might have said that they didn't even know if it was in there, but didn't want to interrupt her flow. She seemed happy just fantasizing about it.

Something else stopped her—a voice shouting from a distance.

"Help! Help! Don't leave! Please don't leave!"

They stopped their bikes and saw a disheveled man stumbling their way out of the trees, waving his arms.

"Please!" he cried in a dry, cracked voice. "I'm lost! I've been wandering around in circles for three days."

Jack looked at Weezy. "What do we do?"

"Do? We help him back to town. What else?"

Good question. That pyramid and the tracks, plus the piney, had left him jumpy. Now this stranger wandering out of nowhere. He didn't like it.

And the guy was getting closer.

"What happened, mister?" he called.

"Lost. I've got a Land Rover somewhere. Came out to do some bird-watching and got turned around and couldn't find my car."

Bird-watcher? Yeah, a lot of bird-watchers in the Pines, but usually in groups. No binoculars around his neck. He could have lost them, but . . .

Jack was liking this less and less. He studied the man, closer now, and could see he looked maybe forty, fifty tops. He needed a shave, his shirt was torn, and his pants were filthy. His longish brown hair was all tangled.

Jack looked at Weezy. "Be ready to ride."

"What's the matter, Jack? You're acting all strange."

"Just being careful is all."

Her expression turned concerned as he unlocked his bike chain and unwound it from the seat pole.

"He's in trouble, Jack. We've got to help him."

"We will. But of all people, you, the Queen of Conspiracies, should know things aren't always what they seem."

The man stumbled onto the firebreak trail. He had a wild look in his blue eyes.

"Thank God! You don't know what I've been through!"

Keeping a tight grip on the chain, Jack said, "You must be thirsty."

"Like you wouldn't believe. Found a pond of cedar water yesterday but nothing since. You kids got anything—a soda, maybe? Anything?"

"Sorry. Come on. We'll lead you back."

"Where?"

"Johnson."

"Never heard of it. Far?"

"Couple of miles that way," Weezy said, pointing west.

He looked at her. "I don't know if I can make it. Think one of you could ride into town and send a cop or an ambulance back?"

Dream on, Jack thought.

"We'll both go. You just wait here and—"

He waved his hands and began walking. "No-no. I don't want to even think about being left alone again. I'll make it. Besides . . ." He looked around. "I don't want to run into that thing again. Ever."

"What thing?" Weezy said as they began to push their bikes, pacing him.

Jack positioned himself between the guy and Weezy. If he went for her, he'd have to go through Jack. And Jack had his chain.

"I don't know. I heard something pushing through the brush last night and thought it was another human. I was about to give it a shout when I heard it make a sound like a hiss. Right then I knew it wasn't human. Or if it was, not any human I wanted anything to do with. Suddenly it seemed to catch on that I was there. It let out this ungodly screech and started charging my way."

Jack saw Weezy's eyes widen—she lived for this stuff—and he knew she was thinking about the tracks around the pyramid.

"What did it look like?" she said.

"I didn't wait to see. I ran."

"Obviously you won the race," Jack said. Otherwise he wouldn't be here to tell his tale.

He shook his head. "I might have in my college days, but I'm way out of shape. No, I got smart and climbed a tree."

"And the thing couldn't climb?" Jack was having trouble buying into this.

"Unfortunately it could."

Weezy said, "Then how—?"

"It was heavier than me—a good deal heavier. I was climbing as fast as I could and it was right behind me and gaining when I heard branches start to crack, then break. I kept going until branches started breaking under my own weight. I stopped—I had no choice. I looked down."

"What did it look like?" Weezy repeated.

He shook his head again. "Couldn't tell you. The sky was overcast—no moon, no stars. The only thing I could see was this dark blob maybe ten feet below me, screeching and clawing at the bark. Then it stopped clawing and started shaking the tree. I tell you, I had to hold on for dear life."

"How'd you get away?"

"I didn't. I mean, I'm here now, but not because of anything else I did. The thing howled and shook the tree for what seemed like forever. Then it finally quieted and climbed down. I prayed it would move on but it didn't. It dug up some sort of stone and started slamming it against the tree trunk again and again. I realized it was trying to cut it down."

"Ohmygod, you must have been scared out of your mind."

"Scared? I damn near shi—" He cut off as he glanced at Weezy. "I was the most scared I've ever been in my whole life."

Jack relaxed his grip on the chain. Maybe this guy was all right.

"So I just hung on all night, rain and all. As the sky began to lighten, the banging stopped. The thing gave the tree one last shake, let loose with one more scream, and disappeared into the trees. But I wasn't going to be fooled. I stayed where I was until it was full light. I wished I could have seen the sun itself, but the dawn gave me an idea where east was, so I climbed down and started walking. I knew if I kept walking east I'd eventually hit the Parkway."

"But you were heading west when we saw you."

He stopped and shook his head. "I guess I was."

Jack pointed up at the thick low clouds. "That's what a vanilla sky will do to you."

"Vanilla sky?"

Jack nodded. "Yeah. Overcast and all one color. And since the Barrens are mostly flat with no landmarks, people get lost all the time."

"Vanilla sky . . ." He looked up. "That's why I haven't been able to find my way out of here. Damn clouds. If you don't know where the sun is, you can't tell your directions."

"That's why they make compasses," Jack said.

The guy didn't appreciate the remark. He gave Jack a look. "I know that, kid."

"There's always moss," Weezy said.

He frowned. "Moss?"

"Sure. Check tree trunks for moss. It's always thickest on the north face."

"Oh, hell!" He slapped a palm against his forehead. "I know that! Or at least I did once. How could I have forgotten? Not that it matters, because I am never, *ever* going in there again."

"Did it stink?" Weezy said. "The thing, I mean?"

The man stared at her. "To high heavens. How did you know?"

Weezy glanced at Jack. "We saw something like that last month."

"Did it come with floating lights?"

Weezy stiffened. "You saw lights?"

"Yeah. When I was parked in that tree. Two glowing blobs, like maybe the size of softballs. They floated along the treetops and circled near me while that thing was bashing the trunk."

"Pine lights," Jack said.

"They're also called lumens," Weezy added.

Jack frowned. "Where's it say that?"

She raised her eyebrows. "I have my sources."

He didn't doubt it. Weezy read stuff hardly anyone else had even heard of.

"They're a kind of ball lightning," he told the man.

He shook his head. "I can't buy that. These things didn't act like any kind of electricity I've ever seen." His expression was unsettled as he looked at Jack and Weezy. "They floated off as the rain began, but as they were hovering there, over me and the beast, I almost got the feeling they were . . . watching."

7

"Oh, thank God!" the man cried as they broke from the trees and the Old Town section of Johnson came into view. "Civilization!"

"Such as it is," Weezy muttered out of the corner of her mouth.

The man dropped to his knees and sobbed.

Jack looked away, embarrassed for him. He'd hoped to find Gus Sooy still here so he could give the man a ride down to the highway where they could call the sheriff's department. But no sign of his battered old pickup. Must have sold off his applejack and gone back to his home in the Pines.

"Only a little farther," Weezy said.

"I can't. I'm all in. Go call for help. I'll wait here. As long as I'm out of those damn woods and can see houses, I'll be okay."

So Jack and Weezy left their bikes and started going door to door, but no one seemed to be home, including Mrs. Clevenger. They didn't try the Klenke house, of course.

"Where is everybody?" he asked Weezy.

She shrugged. "It's a nice day for a change. Maybe they're out catching some rays." She got a funny look in her eyes as she stared over his shoulder. "Let's try . . . there."

He turned and followed her gaze to the boxy, two-story white building that sat on a rise overlooking Quaker Lake—the lake it owned.

"The Lodge?"

"There's a car in front."

True enough. A big gray Bentley limousine was parked by the front entrance. After the murders involving Lodge members last month, two men had moved in. The building had been there as long as anyone could remember, but no one could recall anyone ever living there. Meetings galore, yes, but no residents.

"Tell me you're not thinking what I think you're thinking."

She glanced at him. "Of course I am. This is a golden opportunity. We have a perfectly good reason for asking to use the phone. Once we're inside we can look around for signs of our pyramid. Carpe diem, Jack."

He knew that meant "seize the day." Fine. They could seize the day, but he doubted very much they'd carpe the pyramid.

"Okay. Let's do it. But I'll bet you we don't cross the threshold."

"We have to, Jack." Her tone tightened. "It's ours and they took it."

As they approached the building, Jack realized he'd never been this close. Someone kept it in excellent shape. The stucco walls were clean with no obvious cracks, the paint job fresh looking. The grass needed a good trim, though. And the foundation plantings were looking weedy.

He got a closer look at the big round seal—or *sigil,* as Dad called it—of the Ancient Septimus Fraternal Order over the pillared front entrance.

Jack had always found its eye-crossing design vaguely disturbing. As he stared at it he thought he saw a face appear in one of the windows above it, but it disappeared so quickly he wasn't sure if it had been real or a trick of the light.

"All right," he said in a low voice. "Let me do the talking."

"You don't trust me?"

"Let's just say you're not the greatest at hiding your feelings."

He knocked on the door and realized it was steel. After ten seconds with no response, he was reaching out for another go when it opened. A thick-bodied, thick-necked man with reddish crew-cut hair stared down at them. He wore some sort of butler getup.

"May I help you?" he said with a German accent.

"May we come in and use your phone?" Jack said, pouring on humble politeness. "We need to call the police."

"The Order's phones are not for public use."

As the man started to close the door a voice from within said, "Come, come, Eggers." It carried just a hint of an accent. Perhaps German as well? "Someone must need help."

As the door opened wider, the butler stepped back to be replaced by a tall thin man all in white—white suit, white shirt, white tie. He had a tight-skinned face with a high forehead and a hook nose. His shiny black hair started with a widow's peak and was slicked straight back. His cold blue eyes fixed on Jack as his thin lips curved into a smile. Jack had seen him from a distance when he'd moved in last month.

"You're the young man who found poor brother Boruff's body, aren't you."

Jack nodded, his mouth suddenly dry. He didn't like the idea of this strange man knowing things about him.

The man extended his hand. "How may we help?"

Jack thought he was offering to shake but then noticed he held a white business card between his index and middle fingers. Jack took it.

ERNST DREXLER II
Actuator
ASFO

He had no idea what an *actuator* did, and wasn't about to ask.

"We found a guy who's been lost in the Pines for three days. He's really weak and needs an ambulance."

Mr. Drexler stared at Jack a moment, as if processing the information.

"If we could just come in and use the phone to call nine-one-one—"

"By all means." But instead of stepping aside, he turned and spoke over his shoulder. "Eggers, call the sheriff and tell them to send an ambulance." He turned back to Jack. "Do you know that your father was extended the privilege of joining the Order, yet he turned us down? That does not happen very often."

"He mentioned it."

"Did he mention why?"

"Something about too many secrets."

"'Too many'?" Mr. Drexler frowned. "What an entertaining concept. Just when does one reach the point of 'too many' secrets? Everyone has secrets. Even you." He turned to Weezy. "Even this young lady."

Weezy swallowed. "Wh-what do you mean?"

"You're the young lady who found that strange artifact in the Barrens, aren't you."

With mention of the artifact, Weezy changed, losing her flustered look and switching to angry.

"The artifact you people stole."

Swell, Jack thought. No way we'll get in now.

Mr. Drexler's eyebrows rose as he smiled. "Stole? And why would the Order want something you found buried in the dirt? I'm afraid I've never even read or heard a description of the object. Would you care to describe it for me?"

"You know *exactly* what it looks like."

"Do I? 'Artifact' is such a vague term—it could be anything. But if you won't describe it, can you perhaps tell me what it might be used for?"

Weezy frowned. "Used?"

"Yes. What did it *do*?"

"It didn't do anything that we know of."

"Then what possible use could it be to the Order? Why would we want to . . . steal it?"

Her voice rose. "Because it's proof that there's a Secret History of the World, something your order and other groups like it want to remain secret!"

As Mr. Drexler's smile broadened while he stared at Weezy, Jack edged to the left for a peek through the doors. He saw fringed rugs on the floor—Persian carpets?—dark, indistinct paintings on the walls, a large fireplace with a lot of curios set on the mantel above it. The one in the center looked—

Jack felt his neck muscles bunch as he took a step closer for a better view.

Eggers reappeared then, frowning at Jack as he blocked the space.

But not before Jack spotted a black object similar in size to the pyramid he and Weezy had found—the one that disappeared. This thing seemed to have a pointed top.

Their pyramid?

He hid the thrill jolting through his nerves as Mr. Drexler turned to him.

"Your friend is a most entertaining young lady. I would love to stand here and discuss her Secret History of the World and other wild imaginings, but duty calls." He lifted his gaze and inclined his head toward a place somewhere behind them. "And besides, your lost man is up and about."

Jack turned and saw the man staggering along Quakerton Road toward the bridge. He heard a click and turned back to see the Lodge door had closed. It appeared Mr. Drexler was done with them. Perhaps they'd stopped being "entertaining."

"No!" Weezy cried as she started banging on the door. Her features were tight and her eyes wild. "Open up! Let us in!"

He touched her arm. "That's not going to help."

For an instant she looked as if she was going to pound on him instead of the door, then her shoulders slumped and she nodded. He was afraid she was going to cry, but she took a breath and started down the walk.

"Let's go."

He'd never seen her like this. What was with her, anyway?

8

They caught up to the lost man at the edge of the swollen lake.

"Where're you going?" Jack said.

"Thirsty." He looked at them with glazed eyes, then pointed at Quaker Lake. "Need a drink."

"That's probably not such a good idea," Weezy said. She seemed back in control again. "Might make you sick."

"Come on." Jack pointed to the bridge. "Let's get you across. There's an ambulance on the way."

A sheriff's cruiser pulled up just as they reached the other side. Deputy Tim Davis hopped out and helped the man to the car where he sat on the rear seat with his legs outside and his feet on the ground.

"The ambulance will be here in a few minutes."

After handing him a bottle of water, with advice to drink slowly, Tim turned to Jack. He'd dated Jack's sister, Kate, in high school, so they knew each other pretty well.

"Where'd you find him?"

"He sort of found us."

"That's not answering the question."

Jack glanced at Weezy and said, "Out by Old Man Foster's."

Tim didn't look surprised. "That wouldn't be the land that's posted for 'No Trespassing,' would it?"

"Good thing we just happened by, huh?" Jack added a grin.

Tim didn't return the smile. He looked tense. "I suppose so. Don't go anywhere. I need to talk to you two."

"About what?" Weezy said.

"About the woods."

"Why us?"

"Because you spend so much time there, you should be made honorary pineys."

Ordinarily he might have smiled when he said something like that, but his expression remained grim. Jack wondered what was going on.

As Tim took out his notepad and began asking the man questions, Jack started pulling Weezy aside to tell her what he'd seen on the Lodge's mantel. But then he heard the first question and it puzzled him.

"You didn't happen to see a little boy in there this morning?"

The man shook his head. "I didn't see anyone until I came upon these two."

Tim looked at them. "How about it? Did you see a kid?"

Jack shook his head and saw Weezy doing the same. "No, but—"

But Tim had turned back to the man. He said his name was Ted Collingswood, a broker in the Princeton Merrill Lynch office. He'd arrived in the Pines on Thursday, planning to spend a few days birding. He wasn't due back till today, so nobody would have reported him missing yet. According to his story, Jack estimated he was now at least fifteen miles from where he'd left his car.

By the time he started telling his tale of being chased up a tree by the "thing," about a dozen people had gathered. Jack shook his head, thinking how it didn't take much to draw a crowd in Johnson, New Jersey, the most boring town on Earth.

"Sounds like the Jersey Devil," someone said.

Jack looked but it wasn't Eddie.

Tim said, "Sounds more like a bear."

"Bear?" someone else said. "There ain't no bears in the Pines."

"Yes, there are," Tim said. "We've got black bears. Not a lot, but we've got some, and this man was unlucky enough to stumble across one in the dark. Let's leave it at that, shall we? Let's not start getting all *Twilight Zone* about this. Bears can climb, and they're heavy enough to break branches a man's weight won't."

A bear worked for Jack, maybe even explained the tracks around the pyramid.

Everyone turned then at the sound of a siren as an ambulance roared up Quakerton Road. They watched the EMTs load Mr. Collingswood into the back and roar away.

And as it did, another sheriff's department cruiser pulled up and a deputy got out. Jack didn't recognize him and couldn't read his name-tag from here. After a whispered conversation with Tim, the new deputy leaned back against his car with his arms folded across his chest.

Tim was reaching into a button-down breast pocket of his dark blue shirt as he approached Jack and Weezy.

"We've got a serious situation here, and I'm hoping you can help."

Uh-oh.

"Sure," Jack said. "What's up?"

Tim pulled out a photo and handed it to them.

"Know who this is?"

Jack's stomach clenched when he saw the photo of a smiling little boy with shaggy blond hair.

"That's Cody . . . Cody Bockman. What—?"

"He's missing."

"The little guy we saw this morning?" Weezy said.

"You *saw* him?" Tim said.

The other deputy straightened from the cruiser and approached as Jack told of his encounter.

"Last I saw him, he was pedaling toward his house. What happened?"

"According to the father, the kid had just learned to ride his two-wheeler, and was running it up and down their driveway this morning, going from the street to the garage in back. His dad went in to refill his coffee, and when he came back out, the kid was gone."

"But where?" Weezy said.

"The dad ran up and down Jefferson and every other street in the neighborhood. Not a sign of him."

Jack drew a map in his head. Jefferson was his street. Its west end stopped at the buffer woods along 206. The east end stopped at—

"The lake!"

Weezy's hand shot to her mouth. "Oh, no!"

Tim nodded, his expression even more grim. "That's a big worry. The good news is, we've searched the bank and haven't found any sign of him or his bike. Still . . ."

"There's that circus too," the other deputy said. "A bunch of trucks and trailers and RVs arrived last night."

"You don't really think he ran away to join the circus?" Weezy said.

Jack's throat tightened as he remembered threatening to sell Cody to the circus.

The deputy made a face. "Not likely, but some real shady types in that crew."

Jack said, "I kidded him about that and he seemed to think it was a cool idea."

"We'll check it out," Tim said. "But they're setting up half a mile north on the highway. I don't see a five-year-old who's just learned to ride without his training wheels making his way anywhere near there." He looked down at his pad where he'd taken notes on the lost man. "That Collingswood guy . . . he shows up out of nowhere just after Cody disappears. Could be coincidence, but I don't like coincidences."

"I'm sure he'll turn up," Weezy said.

"Let's hope so. We've been asking everyone we can find if they saw a little kid riding a brand-new, bright red bike. Walt says he thinks he saw a kid riding a red bike into the Pines."

"Thinks?" Weezy said. "Did the kid he saw have blond hair?"

"You know Walt. He says he wasn't paying much attention, and even if he was, I don't know how reliable he'd be. He was in his usual state."

Weezy's expression became defensive.

"Even in his 'usual state' he knows what's going on around town."

Tim shrugged and looked around. "In all fairness, with this being the first dry Saturday in a while, and with so many kids on bikes around here, you'd have to be looking for a specific kid to be able to spot him."

His gaze ranged back and forth, pausing on each of them.

"You two were just in there. Think hard: Did one of you see even a hint of a little kid on a bike?"

Weezy shook her head as Jack said, "I know Cody. If I'd seen him, I'd've grabbed him."

Still, he felt bad now for not following him home.

Tim banged a fist on the fender of his car. "Damn! It was a long shot, but still . . ."

"That doesn't mean he's not in there," Jack added. "He wouldn't have gotten as far in as we were. You know how those firebreaks fork left and right all the time, even close in. He could be just a quarter mile from here but totally lost."

"And unless you know your way," Weezy added, "or know enough to follow your tire tracks back, you can get lost in no time."

Jack had a sinking feeling. "And *stay* lost."

He thought about the day ahead of him. He was supposed to put in a few hours at USED, but he was pretty sure Mr. Rosen would let him off if he asked—especially if it concerned a missing child.

He turned to Tim. "We'll go back in and ride around to see if we can find him."

Tim shook his head. "I'd get my head handed to me for putting even more kids at risk of getting lost."

Weezy looked offended. "We wouldn't get lost."

Tim nodded. "*I* know that, and *you* know that, but the sheriff wouldn't see it that way. Besides, he doesn't want any more bikes in there tracking up the trails."

Jack thought that was stupid. They'd be able to spot Cody's bike tracks before anyone else. And they wouldn't get lost. Weezy could ride a new path and remember everything about it, then add it to the map she kept in her head. Day or night, she knew exactly where she was in the Pines.

Jack was less sure about himself. Certain trails he knew by heart, but he'd never be as at home in there as Weezy.

The trails forked no matter which direction you were moving. You might try memorizing your turns on your trip in, but everything looked different on the way back. Choose one wrong fork and you could wind up in unfamiliar territory, miles from where you planned to be.

Retracing your own tracks was the best way, and promised to be pretty easy today—all the recent rains had smoothed out the sandy surfaces of the trails, leaving them blank, like new sheets of paper waiting for someone to write on them. Perfect for finding Cody's tracks.

Jack was opening his mouth to protest when a flash of light flickered to the west. He saw the underbellies of storm clouds darkening the overcast. Thunder rumbled a few seconds later.

Tim gave his fender an annoyed slap. "Just what we need. Another storm. Perfect timing. Damn!" He turned to Jack. "All right, you guys, head home before it gets here."

Shoving his smarter instincts aside, Jack said, "Let us ride in for a quick look before the storm wipes out all the tracks."

Tim shook his head. "No way. And you know better than that, Jack. The Barrens are the last place you want to be in a thunderstorm."

"But maybe we can pick up his trail. Once the rain comes through, it'll be gone."

"I know that, and I appreciate the offer, believe me. But I've got my orders, and even if I didn't, I'd never forgive myself if I let you kids go in there and something happened. We'll take the cars in and cover as much ground as we can. But as for you two . . ." He jerked his thumb over his shoulder. "Home. Now. Git."

They got.

Guilt followed Jack all the way home. He should have

made sure Cody had got back to his house. If only he'd seen him all the way home and told his folks that he'd been out in the street. But he'd watched him turn onto Jefferson, and hadn't wanted to get him in trouble. All he could think about was that little kid out in the Pines, lost and alone. He could imagine how scared he had to be. And then to be caught in a thunderstorm . . .

Poor kid.

9

That evening, Jack and Weezy were biking north on Route 206 under a clear sky.

The storm had broken hard and mean just minutes after he'd reached his house. Mr. Rosen had called from USED to tell him not to bother coming in—the storm would keep away any potential customers. So he'd spent the afternoon with his father and his frantic mother.

She'd heard about Cody Bockman and hadn't been able to sit still. She kept wanting to get an umbrella and go out searching for him in the storm. It never reached the point where Dad physically had to restrain her, but it had gotten close.

Jack felt the same way. Maybe worse. Should have seen Cody home. The kid must have kept on riding right past his house to who knew where.

The storm blew off to the east about five o'clock. As soon as the rain stopped, Mom dragged his father into the car to drive around, looking.

Jack had gone over to Eddie and Weezy's and they'd biked toward the Pines for their own search. But a deputy had waved them off, saying they didn't want fresh bike tracks messing up the trails.

Jack told him they weren't going to find anything old after the way it had rained, but his arguments fell on deaf ears.

As they'd ridden back through Old Town, Weezy suggested they go watch the circus set up. Eddie begged off—not interested. Jack knew he didn't want to make the trip up 206.

"I think I saw the pyramid," Jack said as they neared the field where the circus set up every year.

Weezy nearly fell off her bike as she gave him a wide-eyed stare.

"You *what*? W-w-when? How?"

"Today, when we were talking to Mister Drexler."

"And you didn't *tell* me?"

"I haven't had a chance. And hearing about Cody pretty much blew it out of my head until now."

"Oh, yeah. I can see that." She brightened. "But the pyramid—you think it's ours?"

He realized she was changing what he said.

"I said I *thought* I'd seen something that might be it. Not even sure it was a pyramid, just looked like—"

"But it could have been."

"Yeah, but—"

She skidded to a halt. Jack stopped a few feet ahead of her.

"We're going back."

He stared at her. "And do what?"

"Find a way into the Lodge and get my pyramid back. I found it and—"

"*We* found it."

"Okay, *we* found it. It's *our* pyramid. And if *our* pyramid is in there, *we* are going to get it back."

He wished he'd never mentioned it.

"I can't believe I'm saying this to you of all people, but you're not thinking, Weez. Think: steel door, barred windows . . . even if we got in we'd be risking more trouble than it's worth."

"Not to me."

"It's worth ending up in jail?"

"It's proof."

"Proof of what?"

"That I'm not crazy."

"Nobody thinks you're crazy."

Deep hurt peeked through her eyes. "Yeah, they do."

Jack realized with a pang that she was talking about her folks, probably Eddie too.

"Well, if that's true, you'll only prove them right by getting caught trying to break into the Lodge." That seemed to sink in, so he pressed it. "Look, let's give it some time, put it on a back burner. Maybe we can come up with something that won't land us in the backseat of Tim's patrol car."

She looked away, then sighed. "Okay. For now. But promise me you'll find a way in, because if you think I'm going to drop this, you're wrong."

Jack had no illusions on that count.

10

A little farther north they came upon a scene of furious activity. The circus had chosen a spot halfway between the highway and the tree line that flowed into the Barrens. Seedy-looking roustabouts were rushing around, unloading trucks, assembling amusement rides, and raising tents. The show's one elephant trumpeted now and again as it hauled stuff through the mud; shouts and chatter and the clang of sledgehammers on spikes filled the air.

Jack guessed the storm had put them behind schedule. The field was quickly becoming a mud pie.

"They call these little circuses 'mud shows,'" Weezy said. "Now I can see why."

"More like a mud bath. People better wear boots tomorrow."

Weezy laughed. "Yeah. Waders."

They stood in silence awhile, staring at the anthill activity.

Finally Weezy said, "I was thinking about what the deputy said—about Cody and the circus. He called them 'shady types.' You think they might have anything to do with him disappearing?"

"You mean kidnapping?"

She shrugged. "I don't know. These mud shows usually hire their roustabouts from homeless shelters and skid-row hotels. Lots of them are alcoholics and druggies."

Jack looked at her. "And you know this how?" When Weezy gave him a *duh* look, Jack said, "Never mind. Silly question."

Weezy had read it somewhere, which meant it was carved on her brain. She never seemed to forget anything she read.

At least she wasn't talking about the pyramid.

Jack watched the workers. Were they really the lowlifes Weezy had read about? Even if so, would they kidnap a kid? What for?

Jack didn't want to think about that.

"Hey, you two," said a phlegmy voice to their right.

Jack saw a skinny guy walking their way. He wore a blue T-shirt with multiple salt-caked sweat rings, ripped jeans, and mud-crusted sneakers. A hand-rolled cigarette dangled from his lips. Lank, greasy hair, an unshaven face, tattoos, an earring, and a lot of missing teeth completed the picture.

Weezy took a quick step back as the guy stopped before them. "We're just watching."

"I can see that. How'd you like to do more'n watch? I'm talkin' work. I'm the canvas boss. We're shorthanded and short on time. Give you free passes to the tent show if you help out."

"No thanks," Weezy said without a second's hesitation.

"I didn't mean you." He focused on Jack. "How about you? Want some passes?"

Jack hesitated, but not because the free passes were tempting—they weren't. He was thinking about Cody. A circus, full of seedy types like this guy, rolls into town Friday night and the very next morning Cody goes missing.

Coincidence? Could be. Most likely was. Just like Mr. Collingswood's appearance. But there was always the possibility . . .

If Jack hired on, it would afford him a chance to look around the circus, see things in an unguarded state, before everything was set up and ready for the public eye.

No. Crazy. That was dumb boy-detective stuff. Like the guilty party—if one existed—would let Cody be seen. Besides, if the sheriff's department hadn't checked out the circus folk already, they soon would.

But it wouldn't hurt to mention Cody to this guy and see how he reacted.

"Nah," Jack said, knocking back his bike's kickstand, "I've got to get back and help search for a missing kid."

The guy stiffened. "Missing kid? What missing kid?"

"A five-year-old boy disappeared this morning."

He threw his cigarette down and ground it viciously into the wet ground.

"Not again!"

This wasn't the reaction Jack had expected.

"Again?"

"Some kid took a powder at one of our stops in Michigan during the summer. What a mess that was."

"Did they find him?"

"Don't know. Didn't know nothin' about that kid." He glared at Jack. "And I don't know nothin' about this one. Don't know nothin' about nothin', okay? None of us do. But sure as hell you townies will think we do, just like the rubes in Michigan. Never fails. Somethin' goes wrong in a town while we're around, and we automatically get the blame." He put his hands on his hips and stared around. "A missing kid! As if this Jonah's-luck weather ain't trouble enough, now this. *Damn!*"

He stormed away without a backward glance.

"Well-well-well," Weezy said. "That sure set him off."

Jack thought he'd looked anything but guilty. But the fact that another kid had disappeared along their route was disturbing. Maybe that guy didn't know anything about it himself, but he couldn't very well know everything his hirelings did in their spare time.

One of the circus folk could be some sort of perv. Jack shuddered at the thought of Cody in the clutches of a child molester.

Suddenly he wanted to be home.

"Let's get out of here."

11

Weezy peeled off at Adams Street and Jack continued on alone to Jefferson and home where he found a strange car parked in the driveway. He stowed his bike in the garage and went in through the back door.

Inside he found the kitchen table set for dinner but no one there. He heard voices from the front of the house and headed that way. In the living room he found three adults and a child: his folks, plus Mr. Vivino and his daughter Sally.

"Hey, Jack," Mr. Vivino said, rising and holding out his hand. He was heavyset with a round face and longish brown hair. "Long time no see."

Jack gave his hand a firm shake, just as he'd been taught to do. His father had told him wimpy men gave wimpy handshakes.

"Hi, Mister Vivino." He turned to the five-year-old girl. "Hey, Sally. How's it going?"

"Okay," she said, barely making eye contact.

And no smile. Sally used to have one of the biggest, brightest, sweetest smiles. Where had it gone?

Jack thought he knew: It left with her brother.

Weezy was pretty much Jack's best friend now, and Kate had been his best friend growing up. But from age eight or nine until twelve, Jack and Tony Vivino had been near inseparable.

Then Tony died.

It started with a broken leg from just hopping over a tree

trunk. No way that little jump should have broken his leg. Something was wrong.

Very wrong. He had some sort of bone cancer that had already spread through his system. They cut off his leg, filled him with drugs that made his hair fall out, and then he died anyway. Jack had cried like a baby. He went to the funeral and hadn't been back to the Vivinos' since. Hadn't seen any of them until last month when Mrs. Vivino and Sally, who'd started kindergarten this year, began showing up at the school bus stop.

He remembered the old days when he'd tickle her just to see that smile. Jack had recovered from Tony's death. It didn't look like Sally had.

"Mister Vivino's running for freeholder," Mom said with a smile of her own.

People told Jack he had the same hair and eyes as his mother. She used to be thin but had added pounds the past few years. Dad didn't seem to mind but she was always complaining about it.

Her smile looked forced and Jack could guess why: no word on Cody Bockman.

"That's great," Jack said to Mr. Vivino. "Can I ask a dumb question?"

He grinned. "The only dumb question is the one that doesn't get asked."

"Okay. What's a freeholder do?"

Mr. Vivino laughed. "They run the county. Mister Haskins's unfortunate death left a gap I'm ready to fill."

The mention of Mr. Haskins changed the mood in the room and triggered uneasy memories. He'd been one of the Lodge members who'd died so mysteriously last month. No one could say for sure whether he'd been murdered, but it was suspected. Stuff like that just didn't happen around here.

Mr. Vivino cleared his throat. "His term was about to expire this year so I'm running to take his place. I'm here to ask your folks for their support."

"And you've got it, Al," Jack's father said, rising from his chair and extending his hand.

No surprise there. His father and Mr. Vivino—his first name was Aldo but everyone called him Al—were both members of the local Veterans of Foreign Wars post. Dad's war had been in Korea. Tony's father was a Vietnam vet like Walt. They'd both come back in one piece—at least physically—but Mr. Vivino worked for an engineering firm in Cherry Hill while Walt . . . well, Walt spent his time being Weird Walt.

Jack's dad was trim, with blue eyes and thinning hair. He held his steel-rimmed reading glasses in his free hand. Jack realized the rising, the handshake, and the promise of support were a subtle heave-ho. Dad was probably hungry.

"Mine too," Mom said.

Jack could tell she wanted to get dinner on the table.

Thankfully Mr. Vivino picked up on it.

"Tom and Jane, I appreciate that." He shook Mom's hand. "I'd be honored if you'd allow me to put a sign up on your lawn."

"Sure," Dad said. "Be our guest."

Jack could almost hear him thinking, *Anything. Just go.*

Mr. Vivino shook Jack's hand again, then led Sally out by the hand.

"Bye, Sally."

Sally looked up and gave him a little wave as she followed her father out. Still no smile.

Jack wished he knew a way to change that. He wished something else . . .

"I wish I could vote," he said as he followed his folks to the kitchen.

"So you could vote for Al?"

"Yeah."

"Why?"

"'Cause he's Tony's father."

Or should that be *was* Tony's father? he wondered.

He guessed he'd always be Tony's father.

"I guess that's as good a reason as any to vote for a freeholder. There's five of them, so any bad apple that happens to land in that barrel can't do much damage."

That brought Jack up short.

"You think he's a bad apple?"

Dad laughed. "Not at all. No, I'm just saying the freeholder system tends to keep things running smoothly. I think Al will be a good addition."

"Why?"

"Well, partly because of Tony. He was a good kid, and I think that says something about his father."

Jack felt his throat constrict. He hadn't thought about Tony in a long time.

He remembered the long summer days they'd spent in the Vivinos' backyard pool, the two of them cannonballing while an ever-smiling Sally paddled around in her floater vest.

Good times.

Then he remembered the wake and seeing Tony in his coffin looking like a shrunken wax doll.

"You miss him, don't you," Dad said.

Jack nodded, unable to speak around the sudden lump in his throat.

Yeah, he missed Tony. Until this moment he hadn't realized how much.

12

That night he dreamed of Tony's wake.

Lightning strobed the sky as he ran through the rain to the front door of the funeral home.

Inside, he pushed through a crowd of adults in dark suits and dresses. They were drinking and talking and laughing while waitresses passed among them with trays of canapés.

What's going on? he thought. This isn't a party. A kid is dead, robbed of his entire life. How can you be happy? How can you laugh?

Worse than that, they were ignoring Tony.

Jack wove through them until he came within sight of the coffin. The lights flickered as the storm lit and rattled the windows. He stopped, afraid to move closer. But he forced one foot in front of the other until he was standing by the kneeler before the coffin.

The top was open and Tony lay within, dressed in his Little League uniform with his first baseman's glove and a ball tucked in beside him. He'd loved baseball.

Another flash and the lights went out. The people behind Jack went on talking and laughing as if nothing had happened. But Jack stood rooted to the spot, unable to speak or move.

Still another lightning flash, but this one kept flickering, revealing Tony sitting up in the coffin and staring at him with pitch-black eyes.

"Save them, Jack. I can't do it, so you've gotta. Save them."

And then the lights came back on, but not in the funeral home—

—in Jack's bedroom.

He blinked up at his mother and father standing over his bed.

"What? Where?"

"That must have been one hell of a nightmare," his father said.

"Nightmare?"

"Screaming like a banshee."

"Are you okay?" his mother said, concern large on her face. "You sounded so frightened."

"I guess I was. Tony was in the dream."

Dad nodded. "No stretch as to why you were dreaming about him."

Yeah. Of course. Mr. Vivino's visit. But what had Tony meant?

"Save them, Jack. I can't do it, so you've gotta. Save them."

Save whom?

SUNDAY

1

Jack wheeled his bike past the VIVINO FOR FREEHOLDER sign stuck in his front lawn and cruised over to North Franklin. He had no destination in mind, just wanted out of the house for a while before it started raining again. It had rained during the night, so no sense in trying to cut the sodden mess that the lawns would be. He simply rode and thought about his dream last night and the whereabouts of the little black pyramid and what the canvas boss had said about a missing kid in Michigan.

As he approached Quakerton Road, he wondered if Cody had been found. Mom hadn't mentioned him. He supposed someone would have called her, but you never knew. Cody's folks might be so happy to have him back they hadn't got around to spreading the word.

No harm in hoping, he guessed.

But hope was dashed when he reached Quakerton and saw Mrs. Bockman tacking a flyer to one of the utility poles. She wore a pinkish warm-up and sneakers.

He coasted up behind her and got a look at the poster: HAVE YOU SEEN THIS BOY? across the top, and a picture of a smiling, blond-haired kid below—the same photo Tim had shown him yesterday.

Jack didn't know what to say besides, "Can I help?"

She started and turned. Her brown hair was messy, like she hadn't combed it in a while, and her eyes were baggy and bloodshot like she'd been crying instead of sleeping.

"Oh, Jack," she said in a wavery, high-pitched voice. "Have you seen him? Have you seen my Cody?"

"No, ma'am." He hadn't meant to say "ma'am"; it had simply popped out. Maybe because here and now, speaking to this devastated woman, it seemed *right*. "I haven't. But I can help you post those flyers."

She hesitated. "I . . . I don't know. I need to be *doing* something."

"Well, you can be looking for him while I'm doing this. I'll put two on every pole in town—one facing each way."

More hesitation as she stared at him. Then, "You were always nice to Cody, Jack. He looked up to you."

Looked . . . that sounded like she didn't think she'd get him back.

"We'll find him. Let me post those."

"Okay. Every pole in town, both sides of the highway, right?"

"Right. Every pole."

She seemed relieved. "Thank you, Jack."

She finished posting the one she'd been working on, then gave him her hammer, a container of tacks, and a box of flyers.

Jack hauled it all back to the Connell house and asked for help. Weezy was on board in a flash. Eddie was griping about not being able to find his *Star Trek* electronic phasers—he'd wanted some target practice—but even he volunteered. They got hammers from their father, split the flyers and tacks with Jack, and were on their way. Weezy took the south side of Quakerton, Eddie the north—because he was already there and wouldn't have to ride far—and Jack took Old Town.

As he passed the Lodge he had an idea. He coasted up the walk and knocked.

The man called Eggers, dressed in his all-purpose dark uniform, answered. He didn't know if Eggers was a first name or last. Not sure of his exact function either. He acted as doorman and chauffeur, but Jack wondered if he might be some sort of bodyguard too. He certainly looked powerful enough.

"May I help you?"

"Can I speak to Mister Drexler?"

Jack tried for another view of the mantel as Eggers did a Frankenstein-monster half turn and stepped back, but no luck. Mr. Drexler appeared in the doorway immediately, dressed in his usual immaculate white suit and tie.

"Yes, what is it? I hope you're not collecting for anything."

"It's not about money. It's about a missing boy."

Mr. Drexler's eyes turned to ice. "I've heard about it. Terrible thing. You can't possibly think I know anything about it."

Jack peeled off about a dozen flyers and held them out.

"No way. Why would you? I'm just helping find him. We're hanging up these flyers and I wanted to know if you'd take some."

Mr. Drexler stared at them as if they might carry germs.

"And do what with them? Send Eggers around with a hammer and nails?"

"No, I just thought you might be able to hand them out to some of the Lodge members."

"This is not the VFW or the women's club. We do not

have smokers and don't find tea parties the least bit entertaining."

Whoa. Talk about a cold guy. But Jack wasn't going to back down. He straightened his arm, pushing the flyers closer.

"Well, just in case you see any of your Lodge brothers. You know, just to help out. He's only five."

Mr. Drexler hesitated a second, then snatched the stack from Jack's hand.

"Very well. If I see any. And now, good day."

Some people . . .

As the door began to close, Weezy's words from last night popped into his head.

. . . promise me you'll find a way in, because if you think I'm going to drop this, you're wrong . . .

And with them, an idea.

"Who's doing your lawn?"

"At the moment, no one." Mr. Drexler gave him an appraising look. "It occurs to me that I have on occasion witnessed you riding your bike around town trailing a lawn mower behind you. From that may I infer that you cut lawns?"

"Um . . . you may. Want me to do yours?"

"The local Lodge's landscaper—former landscaper, I should say—has been released for incompetence. More accurately: inattention. I believe in hiring locally, so . . . are you capable?"

Jack did a quick mental calculation. Lots of grass around the Lodge. Easily three times the average lawn, maybe four. What to charge . . . ?

"Absolutely . . . but it's a lot of property . . ."

"We'll pay you fifty dollars a week until frost halts growth. Is that sufficient?"

Sufficient? Was he kidding? Jack charged five bucks for the average forty-five-minute mow. He didn't know what to say.

Mr. Drexler sighed. "Very well, sixty dollars, but that is my final offer."

Jack found his voice. "Deal."

"Excellent."

Mr. Drexler's cold blue eyes fixed on him, and for an instant Jack felt like a field mouse being eyed by a hawk. But the feeling vanished almost as soon as it came.

Rich! He was going to be *rich*! Plus he'd have lots of opportunities for another peek at the mantel.

"I hope you understand," the man added, "that includes weeding the flower beds and such."

"Weeding? Sure."

For sixty bucks, of course he'd weed.

"Good. Now that we've come to terms on that—you drive a hard bargain, my boy—good day."

He closed the door and Jack walked away thinking about how flush he was going to be and how this was a foot in the Lodge's door. He was sure, given enough time, he could work his way inside.

He moved on and attached a flyer to every pole and tree along every street in Old Town. A lot of them already sported posters for the Taber & Son Circus. As he tacked up Cody's picture next to one of those he thought of the canvas boss from last night and what he'd said.

"Again?"

Had there been a connection between the circus and the

boy who had gone missing in Michigan? If so, there definitely could be one with Cody's disappearance.

But what could he do? He was a fourteen-year-old kid. He could do only so much. Tacking up the flyers was something, but didn't seem enough.

Had to be something else. If so, he'd find it.

2

Every so often—like today—Jack got a chance to pick a lock.

After the posters were up, he rode down to USED to see if Mr. Rosen needed him.

"I'm glad you're here," the thin old man said as Jack came through the front door. "We've got a little work to do."

Jack had begun working here last spring. USED sold pretty much anything and everything, as long as it was used. Well, not appliances or anything like that, but all sorts of furniture, books, magazines, toys, dishes, glassware, clothes, whatever. Jack cleaned and dusted, rearranged, and manned the cash register whenever Mr. Rosen took one of his naps in the back room.

A mahogany cabinet stood on gently curving legs near the front counter. Jack hadn't known mahogany from pine when he started, but Mr. Rosen had taught him how to identify all the different furniture woods.

"A fellow brought it in yesterday, just as I was closing," Mr. Rosen said. "He wasn't asking an arm and a leg, so I bought it. A nice piece."

"Nice finish."

Jack spotted a few nicks and scratches, but Mr. Rosen had taught him how to fix those.

The old man pointed to a spot by the left wall.

"I cleared a space for it over there. Help me move it already."

Together they slid it across the floor. Just as they were

shimmying it into place against the wall, the street outside lit up, followed by a rumble of thunder.

"Swell," Jack said. "Another storm."

At least his bike was sheltered under the store's front overhang.

Mr. Rosen stepped to the front window and stared out. "Like cats and dogs it rains. Where will it all go?"

"The lake?"

He turned and looked at Jack. "And after that?"

Jack shrugged.

"I have another job for you," he told Jack as he returned to the cabinet and tugged on its door handles. "It's locked and they lost the key. I'll need you to open it for me."

Jack put on an evil grin and rubbed his hands together. "Goody!"

"You like this lock picking a little too much, I think."

"Like it?" Jack said as he headed toward the rear where they kept the kit. "I *love* it."

And he did. A fair number of the old pieces came locked with no key. Mr. Rosen used to pick the locks, but his hands had become too shaky for the fine manipulations necessary. So this past summer he'd taught Jack the technique. Every lock Jack conquered was a thrill.

"A Willie Sutton I've made."

Jack returned with the kit. "Who's Willie Sutton?"

"A famous bank robber. When he was asked why he robbed banks, he supposedly said, 'Because that's where the money is.'"

Jack laughed. He kind of liked that.

The day grew dark outside as he inserted a tension bar into the cabinet's keyhole and began caressing the lock's internal pins with a slim, curved-tip rake. The lock hadn't been opened in a long time and the pins resisted movement—happy right where they were. He was just coaxing them to move when three things occurred almost simultaneously:

A sun-bright flash, followed instantly by a deafening crackle-roar, and then darkness as the lights went out.

Mr. Rosen groaned. "Another power failure already!"

"Swell," Jack said, feeling around on the floor—he'd jumped and dropped the rake.

He found it and was about to go looking for a flashlight when he realized he didn't need light. Once the tiny tools were in the keyhole, the job was all feel.

He went back to work, teasing the pins into motion. When they were all in place, he twisted the tension bar and was rewarded with a solid *click*.

"Got her!"

He grabbed the knobs but didn't pull.

"Good boy," Mr. Rosen said, approaching with a flashlight. "Wait for me."

This was a game they'd begun to play and, next to the actual picking of the lock, Jack's favorite part. Who knew what lay within a long-locked cabinet or drawer? A skull? An ancient, forbidden book like the *Necronomicon*? A clue to an unsolved crime? So far he'd been frustrated, but you never could tell. The latest could always hold a surprise.

Mr. Rosen trained the beam on the doors.

"All right. Go ahead."

Jack pulled on the knobs and swung the doors open to reveal . . .

Empty shelves.

"Bummer."

The overhead lights came on just as the front door

chimed. Jack went to see who it was. He found a black-haired man in a white suit standing by the counter tapping his silver-headed black cane on the floor. Eggers stood by the door.

"Mister Drexler," Jack said, pretty much at a loss for anything else to say. "What are you doing here?"

"Why, I came for my tango lessons. Why else would I come to a shop called USED?"

"I'm . . . sorry?"

He smiled. "A terribly lame attempt at absurdist humor, I'm afraid. But you did ask a rather inane question."

Jack thought about that, then nodded. "I guess I did."

"I'm glad you see that. Please try to avoid such in the future."

"I'll do my best. Anything I can help you with?"

"Yes. I was passing by and remembered I'd been told you worked here."

Uh-oh. Had he found someone else to do the Lodge's lawn?

"By who?"

"*Whom*. It's 'by *whom*.' And the *whom* doesn't matter." He turned and said, "Eggers, those passes."

The big man stepped forward and handed Mr. Drexler a white envelope, which he in turn handed to Jack.

"Circus passes. I can imagine few things less entertaining than a circus, but I'm sure you'll find it enthralling. Share these with your acquaintances. But in the meantime, find me something . . ." He looked around . . . "Entertaining."

Entertaining . . . what did he mean by *that*?

"Well . . ."

Another flash, another crash, and the lights went out again.

Just then Mr. Rosen arrived from the rear. He stopped when he saw Mr. Drexler. "I've seen you around town, haven't I?"

Mr. Drexler produced a card seemingly from nowhere and placed it on the counter. As Mr. Rosen reached for it, his sleeve rode up, revealing the numbers tattooed on his forearm. He saw Mr. Drexler staring at them.

"You've seen such before?"

Mr. Drexler nodded but said nothing.

"You're too young to have been in the war, but what about your family? Which side?"

Mr. Drexler's eyebrows rose. "My family does not fight in wars. At least not in the kind you mean."

Mr. Rosen picked up the business card and studied it for a few seconds.

"An 'actuator' it says. What exactly do you actuate?"

Mr. Drexler gave one of his thin-lipped smiles. "Whatever requires it."

And now it was Mr. Rosen's turn to stare—at Mr. Drexler's black cane.

"That looks like it's wrapped in leather."

Mr. Drexler's smile broadened. "Leather implies bovine origin." He held up the cane for Mr. Rosen to see. "Nothing so proletarian, I assure you. It's trimmed with black rhinoceros hide."

Mr. Rosen ran a finger along the rough surface.

"How unusual."

"Yes, well, I've never had much use for the usual."

Jack noticed a squiggle atop the silver head.

His gut clenched. He was almost sure it was one of the symbols carved on both the big and little pyramids. He had a copy of all seven symbols hidden in his bedroom. He wished he could run home and check it out.

"You want to sell it?"

Mr. Drexler pulled the cane back. "Most certainly not. This belonged to my father. He too was an actuator."

After another flash and rumble, Mr. Rosen said, "Looks like we'll have no power for a while. I'm afraid I'll have to close up."

Mr. Drexler nodded. "Very well. Some other time, then."

He walked out. As the door closed behind him, Jack peeked into the envelope: four passes to the Taber circus. How did Mr. Drexler come by these? Was there a connection between the circus and the Septimus Order?

"You can't ride your bike in this," Mr. Rosen said. "I'll drive you home."

"Thanks, I—"

He spotted Weird Walt signaling to him through the front window. Jack stepped out to see what he wanted.

Walt wore his uniform of jeans, T-shirt, olive-drab fatigue jacket, and black leather gloves. No one Jack knew had ever seen him without those gloves. Word was he even ate dinner with them. He had a gray-streaked beard, and today he'd tied his long dark hair back in a ponytail, giving him a definite hippie look. His eyes had their customary semi-glaze from applejack. He'd been a medic in Vietnam and had spent time in a V.A. mental hospital after the war. He'd supposedly starred in a faith-healing tent show until he got kicked out for his drinking. A few years ago he landed at his sister's house here in Johnson.

"Hey, Jack."

"Hey, Mister Erskine."

He smiled through the beard. "It's Walt—you know that."

"Okay." Jack had trouble calling a guy nearing forty by his first name. "Looking for anything special?"

"Yeah, in a way. Came to give you a warning—you and Weezy."

Uh-oh.

"Really?"

"Yeah. Stay out of the Pines for a while."

Jack didn't know how to take that.

"What do you mean?"

"I know you and her—especially her—like to go traipsing around in the Barrens, and I heard about you two finding that lost guy, which is all well and good, but not around the equinox."

Right. The autumnal equinox was sometime this week. But . . .

"Why not?"

"Things get a little crazy in there with the fall equinox. It's due on Wednesday, but the hinges start to loosen a few days before, and don't get back on track until a few days after. I was in there yesterday and I could feel it getting strange. Couldn't you?"

Jack shook his head as he shrugged. "No."

He wondered if Walt might have been feeling an excess of applejack.

"Well, anyway, just do yourselves a favor—me too, 'cause I like you kids. Haven't forgot how you took my back last month. Stay outa there till next week, understand?"

Jack straightened and saluted. "Understood."

Walt returned the salute, then said, "You'll tell Weezy, huh?"

"Absolutely."

"Yeah, I was gonna try to catch you guys on the street but Mrs. Clevenger said I should get in here today, right this very minute, and tell you."

Jack thought that if Mrs. Clevenger said so, maybe he'd better listen.

When he went back inside, Mr. Rosen was waiting. Jack spotted Mr. Drexler's card on the counter and remembered what it said.

"What exactly is an 'actuator'?"

"In a mechanical sense," Mr. Rosen said, "it's a piece of equipment that sets things in motion. In a man, who's to say?"

"A guy who sets people in motion?"

He shrugged. "More generally speaking, a man who makes things happen."

Jack looked out the window. What was the Septimus Order's actuator doing in Johnson . . . with a cane topped with a symbol from the pyramids?

Too many connections for comfort.

3

The first thing Jack did after Mr. Rosen dropped him off was go to his bedroom where he knelt before his dresser and pulled out the bottom drawer. In the space beneath lay the Xerox copies Weezy had made of the symbols on the little pyramid—she'd done rubbings before she'd given it over for analysis. That was the last they'd seen of it. She'd made the copies as a backup—in case something happened to the originals. Good thing too: They'd been stolen as well.

She'd been searching ever since for clues to their meaning but had come up empty.

Jack stared at the seven symbols.

He closed his eyes and tried to picture the one he'd seen on the head of Mr. Drexler's cane. No question: the last one.

That clinched it: The Septimus Order was connected to both pyramids. Which added weight to Weezy's claim that they'd had a hand in the little pyramid's disappearance. If he'd really seen a pyramid on the Lodge's mantel yesterday, it might be a duplicate, but Jack had a feeling in his gut it was the same one.

Big question: Tell Weezy or don't?

Might be better to hold off. No need in setting her off

again. But he'd have to tell her about cutting the Lodge's lawn—she'd find out eventually. He hoped she didn't insist on an immediate plan. Lots of potential there. Better to wait and see how things developed. Play it by ear. He'd come up with something, but it had to be good, had to be safe, had to be sure-fire or damn near.

The rain stopped shortly after that. His pent-up energy prompted him to drag his father out to the front yard for a Frisbee toss, which lasted until the disc wound up in one of the trees. His father was about to pull a ladder from the garage when the current came back on. They left the Frisbee and went to watch the game. The Eagles improved to two and one by beating the Broncos.

"Phone, Jack," his mother called from the kitchen. "Mister Rosen."

Mr. Rosen? he thought as he headed for the kitchen. Did he want to reopen the store?

"Jack," Mr. Rosen said. *"I can assume you'll be going down to the store to pick up your bike soon?"*

"Uh-huh."

"Good. When you do, please ride on down to my place. Not only did I forget to tell you that I'll be away next week, I forgot to pay you."

"Oh, yeah. Okay. I'll see you soon."

With a couple of sources of income, especially the nice chunk of change he'd be getting from the Lodge, he wouldn't be hurting if his USED pay was late, but he figured he liked it better in his pocket than Mr. Rosen's.

But Mr. Rosen going away . . . he hadn't taken time off since Jack had begun working at the store.

He left the house at a loping run and reached USED in

no time. He'd broken a good sweat along the way. The sun was out and the air dripped humidity.

He found his bike right where he'd left it. He supposed in another town you might worry if you left your ride unchained and unwatched on the main drag, but that wasn't a problem in Johnson. Locals here looked out for each other.

He hopped on and rode up 206 to Mr. Rosen's place. He lived on the northbound side of the highway in a trailer about halfway between the Quakerton Road blinker and the lot where the circus had set up. Right next door to the Vivino house, as a matter of fact.

As Jack approached he gave in to an impulse to pay a visit. Their two-story colonial wasn't part of any development. It sat alone on a big lot that backed up to an orchard, facing the highway but set back a couple of hundred feet. He saw a car sitting in the driveway so he figured they were home.

He coasted down the long driveway to the front steps where he rang the doorbell. After two tries and no answer, he decided to peek into the backyard in case they were in the pool.

As he approached the six-foot picket fence he heard Sally crying and Mr. Vivino yelling. He hesitated to reach for the gate handle. Instead he peeked through a gap between a couple of slats. He saw Mr. Vivino and Sally standing beside the pool, while Mrs. Vivino waded in the low end.

Mr. Vivino, his belly bulging above his swim trunks, stood over Sally with his hands on his hips looking down at her.

"I asked you a question, young lady. Where is it? You wanted a pink floater tube, I bought you a pink floater tube, I blew it up for you, and now it's gone. Where did you leave it?"

"Right heeeeeeeere!" she wailed, rubbing her teary eyes.

Mr. Vivino made a show of looking around. "Where is it then? Do you see it? I don't. Show me where it is."

"I don't know!"

"You don't? And why—?"

"For heaven's sake, Al!" Mrs. Vivino said from the pool. "Stop browbeating her!"

Mr. Vivino turned and stepped to the edge of the pool. His tone was low and menacing.

"Where do you get off butting in when—?"

"She's only five. Leave her alone."

His face reddening with rage, he jumped into the pool and grabbed his wife by the hair.

"Shut up!" he shouted. "Shut UP!"

And then he pushed her head underwater and held it there. Sally screamed while her mother thrashed and kicked and splashed, trying to come up for air, but Mr. Vivino wouldn't let her. She was thin and he had an easy hundred pounds on her.

The longer he held her under, the more frantic her thrashing became. Jack overcame his shock and was reaching for the gate handle to run in there and shout at him to let her up when he finally released her.

As she straightened, gasping, choking, and gagging, he said, "Don't you ever, *ever* interfere when I'm disciplining my daughter!" He turned and pointed a finger at Sally. "And you stop that crying!"

But Sally couldn't stop. All she could do was cry, "Mommeeeeee!"

Mr. Vivino climbed out of the pool and roughly dragged her by an arm toward the house.

"Stop it, goddamn it! Stop it now!"

But of course she didn't, and so he slapped her on her backside—Jack flinched at the sharp sound of the wet *smack!*—which only made her wail louder.

And as Mrs. V crouched in the pool with her hands over her face, dripping, coughing, sobbing, Jack noticed a dozen bruises on her arms.

Sickened, he forced back a surge of bile as he staggered away from the fence. His knees felt rubbery. He couldn't have seen what he'd just seen. Tony's dad . . . treating Mrs. V and Sally like that. He felt as if he'd just peeked in on someone's nightmare . . . It couldn't be.

But it was. He'd seen what he'd seen and it made him sick.

Made him angry too. Treating little Sally like that . . . the thought of it loosed a cold, raging darkness within him, urging him to hurt, destroy. He wished he were the Hulk—he was sure as hell furious enough to spark the transformation. He imagined himself smashing through the front door and giving Mr. Vivino a megadose of his own medicine—bouncing him off a few walls and then playing Hacky Sack with him.

But he wasn't the Hulk. He was just a skinny kid and he needed to get away from here as quickly as possible so he could blow the whistle on this creep.

4

As Jack raced back toward the highway, he had two choices: turn south toward town or north to Mr. Rosen's. He chose the latter because it was right next door. The sooner he called the cops, the sooner he could put an end to the nightmare in the Vivino house.

He pulled into Mr. Rosen's yard. His trailer sat on a foundation so it looked more like a typical ranch house.

Nothing else about the house or the yard was typical, though. Half a dozen aerials of all different shapes and sizes jutted from his roof, and a huge satellite dish sat in a corner of his front yard, angled toward the sky. Weezy had jokingly said that he must be trying to receive messages from aliens. Well, being Weezy, maybe only half jokingly.

Mr. Rosen must have seen something in Jack's expression when he let him in.

"What's wrong? What happened?"

"Nothing," Jack said as he stepped through the door.

He'd never been inside Mr. Rosen's home. The front room was crammed with electronic equipment. It could have been a Radio Shack.

"Nothing, shmothing. You look like someone stepped on your grave."

Jack felt he had to tell him something.

"I . . . I heard shouting at the Vivinos."

"Oh, them," Mr. Rosen said, waving a hand as he turned away. "Like cats and dogs they fight."

"You mean it happens a lot?"

"All the time."

"Does he beat her?"

He shrugged. "Who's to say? I can't see through walls."

"Did you ever think of calling the police?"

He turned to face Jack. "If she's not calling, why should I? Maybe she thinks nothing's wrong. Maybe she thinks shouting is the way marriage should be. So if I call the cops, and they come, and she tells them nothing's wrong, like a crazy old fool I look. No. I mind my business, just as you should mind yours."

Probably good advice, but Mr. Rosen hadn't seen Sally get slapped, or her mother sobbing in the pool. No way Mrs. V thought nothing was wrong.

He remembered those summer days when she'd always keep drinks and chips and pretzels out by the pool for them, how she'd fix Jack lunch and tousle his hair as he bit into the thick ham-and-cheese sandwiches she made for him. He remembered how thin and hollow-eyed she became when Tony got sick, how she'd never leave his side, how she'd sobbed at his funeral.

Today's sobs mixed with the echoes of those from memory.

Maybe she was too scared to call. Maybe she needed someone to do it for her.

"Can I use your phone?"

Mr. Rosen gave him a long, appraising look, then nodded. "I warned you, but if you must, don't give your name."

"Don't worry."

Jack had already decided to be invisible in this. He had a number of secrets he was keeping. He figured one more wouldn't hurt.

"And don't say where you're calling from. Just say you were passing by and heard screams, then hang up."

"Won't they be able to trace it?"

He shook his head and pointed to an ultramodern, multiline phone on a nearby table.

"Not if you use that."

Then he turned and walked toward the rear of the trailer.

Jack lifted the receiver and dialed 9-1-1.

"Emergency services."

"I think a woman's getting beaten in Johnson. I was passing by and heard her screaming." He gave the Vivino address.

"May I have your name?"

Jack hung up and turned to find Mr. Rosen returning with a pay envelope in his hand.

"You made your call already?"

Jack nodded. "Short and to the point."

"No names?"

"No names."

He shook his head. "I applaud your willingness to do something, but it will not turn out as you hope."

His cynicism surprised Jack. "How can you be so sure?"

He gave a sour smile. "Things rarely do."

"Look. The deputies will come. They'll know someone reported a woman being beaten. They'll ask to speak to Mrs. Vivino. They'll see all those bruises and ask her about them. All she's got to do is point a finger."

"And press charges."

Jack blinked. "Charges?"

"Simply showing bruises isn't enough. She'll have to charge him with battery."

"Well, this will be her chance."

Mr. Rosen shook his head sadly. "You're a good kid, Jack,

and you mean well, but you've got a lot to learn about people and the way the world works."

"I know plenty."

But did he? When he thought about it, what did he really know? He was a small-town kid who listened to music instead of the news, and limited himself pretty much to the newspaper's funny pages. He watched sports and science fiction movies or shoot-'em-ups, and read Stephen King or moldy old pulp magazines like *The Spider* and *The Shadow*.

Maybe Mr. Rosen was right. Johnson, N.J., was like an island in a quiet pond. Maybe he needed to start tuning in to the world around him.

"Here's your week's pay," Mr. Rosen said, handing him the tan envelope. "Not many hours last week, so not much money, I'm afraid. Things wind down after Labor Day. We'll go into October, then I don't think I'll need you till spring. That is, if you want to come back."

"Sure. I'll come back."

He would have preferred to be independently wealthy, but if he had to work, USED was a great place, and Mr. Rosen was an easygoing boss. Plus he paid in cash, which saved Jack the hassle of applying for a Social Security number.

"Good. And as for this week . . ." He held out a set of keys. "Take these."

Jack recognized the keys to the store.

"Didn't you say you'll be away?"

"That's right. I'll be visiting my nephew." He pointed to the keys. "While I'm out of town, I'd like you to open the store for a few hours a day if you can. I left some change in the till in case you happen to sell anything. And if there's a day or two when you can't open up, just swing by and take a look inside."

"Okay." That didn't seem so hard.

"Oh, and keep a record of your hours there and I'll pay you accordingly."

Jack stared at the keys and couldn't help a swell of pride. A big responsibility. But Mr. Rosen must think he was capable enough . . . and trustworthy enough.

"Will do." He looked up at his elderly boss. "Don't worry. I won't let you down."

He smiled. "If I wasn't absolutely sure of that, I'd simply shut down for the week."

Jack looked around at the roomful of electronic equipment—rows of black boxes with dials and red and green lights and glowing meters.

"Can I ask what all this is? Are you transmitting to outer space?"

"No, I'm listening."

Weezy's theory popped into his head. "To aliens?"

He laughed. "To the world."

"Why?"

His smile faded. "To know what's going on. So I won't be surprised again. So events can't take me unawares as they did back in the day when I assumed everything would work out for the best."

Jack frowned. "I don't under—"

His gaze abruptly shifted past Jack to the window. "Well, well. It appears your call sparked a quick response."

Jack turned and saw a sheriff's department cruiser turning into the Vivino driveway.

"Now he'll get it," Jack said.

The old man shook his head. "Remember what I told you: It will not turn out as you hope."

5

To Jack's dismay, Mr. Rosen was right.

From where he crouched at the window at the end of the trailer's front room, Jack watched a deputy he didn't recognize knock on the Vivinos' front door. Mr. Vivino answered and let him in.

Not even ten minutes later the deputy was back outside and shaking hands with the bastard. Jack strained to hear what they were saying but could catch only snatches, mostly Mr. Vivino's loud voice.

"Sorry you had to come out here for nothing . . . probably just some crank . . . guess I have to expect this sort of thing now that I'm becoming a public figure . . . maybe a rival for the freeholder job . . ." He gestured toward Mr. Rosen's trailer and seemed to look straight at Jack, who ducked farther back from the window. "Or maybe that old coot next door."

The deputy said something Jack couldn't hear but it seemed to surprise Mr. Vivino. "A *boy's* voice? Now who the hell . . . ?"

His heart sank as he watched the deputy return to his unit and drive away.

To his credit, Mr. Rosen did not say *I told you so.*

Instead Jack heard the echo of the wet smack of Sally's father's hand against her butt, almost felt its sting, and the anger returned.

Mr. Rosen looked at him and said, "That's a fierce look on your *punim*, young man."

"Punim?"

Mr. Rosen paused, then gave his head a quick shake. "Sorry. I meant *face*. I can tuck the old tongue away in the workaday world, but it slips out at home."

Jack figured if Mr. Rosen could detect a fierce look on his *punim*, he was giving away too much.

"I'm just disappointed, is all. Is that the best they can do?"

"I'm afraid so. And you should think it's for the best that you live in a country where they cannot come and drag you away simply because an anonymous caller said you did something wrong."

"Yeah, I guess so."

"Don't guess so—*know* so." The sudden sharp edge on Mr. Rosen's voice took Jack by surprise. "Take it from someone who once lived in such a place."

"Where?"

He shook his head. "Doesn't matter now. It's gone. But there are other places like it in the world. Be thankful you live here."

Jack was thankful, but that didn't make him any less frustrated. He couldn't bear to think of Sally having to go on living like that day after day. If her big brother were here, he'd do something—maybe take a licking defending her, but he wouldn't have stood by and watched.

Tony, however, was gone.

But Jack wasn't.

He had to do something, had to find a way to bring down Mr. Aldo Vivino. The nerve of the bastard, dragging his daughter around from house to house trying to cadge votes by pretending he was the wonderful family man and loving father. Time to let the world see who he really was.

Jack had tried going through proper channels with no results. Time to try another way.

Jack's way.

6

After dinner, Jack, Eddie, and Weezy rode up to the circus. He found it hard riding past the Vivino house. He got steamed again thinking about what he'd seen.

When they reached the muddy lot, Jack tried to put Sally out of his head and enjoy the show. Wasn't easy. Especially with flyers about the missing Cody all over the place.

Sally . . . Cody . . . was it just him, or was the world becoming a darker place?

He didn't make much progress with his Sally rage until he reached the shooting gallery. The rifles were air-powered and shot pellets instead of bullets, but they *fired*, and that was what counted. He pretended the targets were Mr. Vivino and it took him five magazines before he scored enough hits to feel some relief. If he'd had his own BB gun growing up, he might have scored better, but he'd suffered through a gunless childhood.

"Let's hit the sideshow," Eddie said. "They've got some freaks and stuff."

Jack had never understood the attraction of staring at deformed people, but he did want to see the motorcycle show.

"Hey, Weezy."

Jack turned and saw Carson Toliver approaching.

Swell.

Toliver, a muscular, tanned senior with blond surfer hair, was top dog at South Burlington County Regional High School—captain and quarterback of the Burlington Badgers and last year's high scorer on the basketball team. Girls went gaga over the guy. Weezy was no exception.

"Hi, Carson," she said, a giggle edging into her voice.

For some reason he seemed interested in Weezy, and any contact with him seemed to soften her brain. Jack could almost hear her IQ dropping as she gazed at him.

Toliver pointed down the midway. "C'mon. I want to show you something."

"Okay."

Jack wanted to say that the three of them had always done the circus together, but bit it back. She caught him looking at her.

"What?"

"Nothing," he said. "We'll catch up to you later."

"Okay. You two have fun."

Jeez, it was like he'd just turned into a little brother.

He watched her and Toliver walk away for a few seconds, then turned to Eddie. "Let's do the bumper cars. I feel like crashing into something."

As they waited on line, a guy with a camera came up to them. He had signs pinned front and back on his sweatshirt.

Instant Home Movies!
Only $10!

"You kids want movies of you in the bumper cars?"

"We don't have a projector," Eddie said.

The guy laughed. "You don't need one. Got a VHS player?"

"Sure."

He patted the camera. "This baby records straight to a

videotape. You just take it home and plug it into your VCR. Instant home movies! It's the latest thing!" He looked around. "Where are your folks?"

"Home," Jack said.

The guy frowned. "Got ten bucks?"

Jack shook his head. "Not for a film of me and him."

With an immediate loss of interest, the guy moved on to greener pastures.

Instant home movies, Jack thought. What'll they think of next?

The idea stayed with him through the bumper car ride where he slammed into everyone in sight, and followed him to the end of the midway where they came upon the traditional game of swinging a mallet and trying to ring a bell atop a board.

Three Swings for a Dollar.

Jack wasn't interested. He knew his skinny arms wouldn't be able to power that ringer to the top, and the prize was a teddy bear. Who wanted a teddy bear?

The sun was gone, leaving the circus an island of light in a sea of deepening darkness. Jack glanced toward the trees bordering the field and saw two points of light in the shadow. They blinked off and then on again.

He thought he could make out a hulking shape within the dark. But then the points blinked off and never came on again.

Eyes? Had something been watching the circus from the pines? It couldn't have been a person because human eyes didn't glow like that. And what kind of animal had eyes so far off the ground?

Unless . . .

He shook it off. That was Weezy territory.

They entered the sideshow and ambled past the freaks.

Only half a dozen present if you counted the Siamese Twins as two: Armando the Armless Saxophonist, Corinda the Cow-faced Woman, Tiny the World's Fattest Man, and Peter the Pinnochio Boy who was a midget dancing around with elastic strings stretching from the ceiling to his wrists and ankles.

Jack suspected the Siamese twins were tied at the shoulder rather than truly joined. He was watching them closely, looking for evidence of fakery as they juggled—a clever act—when Eddie hurried up and grabbed his arm.

"Jack," he said, grinning, "you've got to see this thing down here. They're calling it a 'machine' but it doesn't do anything!"

Jack followed him to a stall where an odd gizmo sat on a rotating platform under a hand-printed sign.

THE MYSTERY MACHINE

The weirdest thing Jack had ever seen: a bunch of odd-colored, odd-shaped pieces—flat, round, oval, irregular, opaque, clear like glass—haphazardly stuck together with no rhyme or reason. Like something a toddler would put together from an alien Tinkertoy set.

"Isn't it a riot?" Eddie said. "It just sits there."

He was right. It simply sat and rotated on its stand. Dumb. Jack was turning away when something caught his eye. He turned back and stared. He could have sworn . . .

Nah. Impossible.

He made another move to leave when he saw it again—or thought he did.

For an instant—just an instant—the upper half of one of

the pieces seemed to have faded away. It looked fine now, but Jack was sure . . .

He stared unblinking. If it happened again, he'd catch it.

"What did you see?"

A thin, balding, bookish man to his left had spoken.

"Not sure," Jack said. "More like what I didn't see."

"Something faded in and out of view?"

Jack nodded. "That was how it looked."

"I didn't see anything," Eddie said.

"Only certain people can, and then only out of the corner of the eye."

"What is it?" Eddie said.

The man smiled. "A mystery."

"Yeah, fine. But it says it's a machine. What's it *do*?"

"It fascinates."

"The fading in and out of view," Jack said. "Optical illusion, right?"

The man shrugged. "Perhaps. Or perhaps it goes somewhere."

"'Goes'?"

"As in: leaves here and pokes into another place."

"What other place?"

The man's smile was almost sad. "That's the real mystery. I—"

"Hey, Prather!" someone said, and the man turned.

"Yes?"

The canvas boss from last night walked up and said, "Little Taber wants t'see you."

As the bookish man hurried off, the boss looked at Jack. "Want tickets to the cycle show?"

"Well—" Jack started to say.

"You would've had free passes if you'd pitched in last

night," he said with a sharp grin. "But now you'll have to buy them, won't you?"

Jack pulled out the passes Mr. Drexler had given him. "Not exactly."

The grin vanished. "Where'd you get those?"

"I've got my sources," Jack said, turning away.

"What's he talking about?" Eddie said.

Jack told him, keeping watch on the Mystery Machine as they walked away, but nothing faded away this time.

Pokes into another place . . . yeah, right. An optical illusion and nothing more.

"Any word on that kid?" the boss called after them.

Jack looked back. "Not that I heard."

The guy shook his head in what looked like disgust. "We're doing our part, you know."

"Yeah, I saw the posters."

As he and Eddie continued toward the main tent, Jack was doubly sure that particular roustabout knew nothing. But that didn't mean somebody else here didn't.

One of the freaks, maybe?

Instantly Weezy's voice was in his inner ear: *Oh, sure, blame it on the freaks. Just because they're different doesn't mean they're evil.*

Okay, right, sure. Different didn't equal evil, but that didn't guarantee *not* evil. Maybe if you were treated badly all your life because of a twisted outside, you became twisted inside.

His imagination was running now. What if Peter the Pinnochio Boy pretended to be a little kid—he was small enough to pass—and lured Cody into a trap and—

Jack's mind balked at going any further.

They reached the main tent, showed their passes, and

found seats. After watching the animal show—dopey—and cycle stunts—cool—they wandered back outside.

"Where's your dear sister?" Jack said as he watched some hapless father trying to win a teddy bear for his little girl by throwing darts at balloons.

Why wasn't Mr. Vivino here doing that for Sally? What was wrong with him?

"With Toliver somewhere, I guess," Eddie said.

Jack had had enough so-called fun, and was ready to head home. But they couldn't leave without Weezy.

"Let's go look. You head toward the front, I'll take the rear. We'll meet back here in a couple of minutes."

As he walked along he heard, "Hi, Jack."

He turned and recognized a girl from one of his classes.

"Hi, Karina."

What was her last name? He'd started high school only a couple of weeks ago and hadn't nailed down all the new names yet.

Haddon. That was it. Karina Haddon.

She smiled. "I figured you'd be here, seeing as it's practically in your backyard."

She had a nice smile and wore her dark blond hair short, though not as short as his sister Kate's. She had most of it hidden under a striped engineer's cap now. Her brown eyes sparkled in the lights strung overhead.

He said, "You're from Tabernacle, right?"

Tabernacle was the next town north on 206. Karina was always seated on the school bus beside her friend Cristin by the time Jack boarded. Compared to other girls in the class, she tended to dress down—way down. Like bulky sweaters and loose jeans. Tonight she wore a Bob Marley T-shirt.

She rolled her eyes. "My dad drove me and Cristin and he's been like hanging over us."

"Where is she?"

She looked around. "I'm not sure . . ."

Just then a grinning brunette slipped through a knot of people.

"Hey, you found him," Cristin said.

Jack saw Karina give her a shut-up look.

"Oh, uh, well, your dad's like having a major cow because you wandered off. He wants to find you and skate."

Karina turned to him and said, "Gotta run. See you in school tomorrow."

She waved and hurried off with Cristin, the two of them blabbing a hundred miles an hour.

Hey, you found him.

Had Karina been looking for him?

Interesting, he thought as he resumed the search for Weezy.

He found her standing by the hammer game with two other sophomore girls. Though only four months older, Weezy was a year ahead of Jack in school.

The other two were giggling as they watched Carson Toliver swing the mallet and try to ring the bell atop the board. His muscles bulged beneath his tight T-shirt.

But he wasn't having much luck reaching the bell. Despite pounding the pad on the base pretty hard, he was moving the striker weight only a third or halfway up. Weezy joined the others in calling out the labels on the levels as he reached them.

Whack!

"Wimp!"

Whack!

"Dork!"

Whack!

"Nerd!"

Jack wondered why he felt such pleasure watching him fail. He was supposed to be a pretty nice guy. He'd never picked on Jack—never acted any way toward Jack—but for some reason he disliked the guy.

A word popped into his head.

Jealous?

No way.

Yeah, Weezy had kissed Jack on the lips last month but that hadn't meant anything. Little more than a peck. They weren't like that. They were friends, nothing more.

Still . . . nothing more he'd like to do right now than show up Carson Toliver.

As Jack watched him swing the hammer he noticed how the pad was fixed about four inches in from the outer edge of the rocker board. With that loss of leverage, even Conan the Barbarian would have a tough time ringing the bell.

But if you just so happened to miss the pad and hit the outer edge of the board . . .

He caught Weezy's eye and jerked his thumb toward the front end of the midway. She nodded and held up a finger: *Meet you there in a minute.*

Maybe she didn't want to be seen deserting Toliver for a frosh. Or maybe she thought Toliver was going to try again. But he threw the mallet down instead.

"It's rigged!"

Jack stared at the sign: *Three Swings for a Dollar.* On impulse he pulled out a bill and waved it.

"I'm next!"

The carny running the game took his dollar and pointed to the mallet. As Jack picked it up he saw Weezy standing between the two snickering sophs and giving him a what-are-you-thinking? look.

He gripped the very end of the mallet handle, rested the head on the rocker pad, then stepped back six inches. He raised it high above his head, took a breath, and swung with everything he had—

And missed. The mallet head smacked into the mud with a gushy *thok!*

Jack felt his face heat up as Toliver and the two other girls burst into laughter. Weezy stood with her eyes closed, shaking her head.

The carny gave him a gap-tooth grin as he tapped the rocker pad. "Guess I shoulda told ya. Y'hit 'er here, not the ground."

They laughed louder.

Jack did his best to ignore them as he reset his grip and repeated the same process, except this time he backed up only three inches. Again he raised it high and swung, putting his back as well as his arms into it.

The mallet head caught the outer edge of the board, sending the weight shooting all the way to the top. As the sound of the bell rang through the air, Jack dropped the mallet.

"You don't get no prize," the carny said, "because you didn't hit the pad. Y'gotta hit the pad."

Jack didn't care. He'd just wanted to see if he could do it. He shoved his hands in his pockets and walked away without looking at Weezy and company. Didn't have to. Their silence said it all. He didn't wait for her. It definitely would not be cool for her to walk away with the frosh who'd just one-upped Carson Toliver.

But halfway to the entrance she appeared beside him.

"I saw what you did," she said.

He glanced at her. She was grinning.

"And what would that be?"

"Hit the end of the board. Nerds know levers."

Jack resented that. "Nerd, huh? I guess I left my taped glasses and pocket protector home."

"Maybe nerd's not the right word. How about misfit? You're into things most kids wouldn't understand. Your mind works differently. I should know. I'm the same. But you know how to hide it."

"I don't hide anything."

Well . . . maybe a few things.

"Yeah, you do. You don't even know you do. Kids just think of you as kind of a loner. Me . . . they think I'm weird. But I'm learning how to hide it."

"Why?"

She glanced back at the kids she'd left behind. "Because sometimes I wish . . ."

"Wish you were like them?"

"Not *like* them, exactly. It's just that . . . sometimes I get tired of being on the outside looking in, and I start thinking it might be nice to be on the inside looking out."

"Better view?"

She shrugged. "Maybe. I'd like the chance to compare. You ever feel that way?"

Jack thought about that. It took only a second.

"No."

"Never?"

He shook his head. "Never even occurred to me. And I'm surprised to hear you talking like this. It's not you. You always seemed so . . . happy with who you are."

"Happy?" She looked away. "I don't know if I've ever been happy."

"Sure you have."

"Okay. Yes. I was happiest when I had the pyramid. And I was happy just now to see you ring that bell." She gave him a gentle punch on the shoulder. "Brain beats brawn every time, right?"

"Not every time, but it's got a good win-loss record."

She heaved a theatrical sigh and slipped her arm through his as they walked.

"My hero."

He had to laugh at her unpredictability. Her warm skin tingled against his and made for a nice end to a mostly crappy day.

I was happiest when I had the pyramid.

Really? Then Jack was going to get it back for her, one way or another.

MONDAY

1

Jack's father slammed on the brakes in their driveway.

"What the hell?"

He'd been leaving for work the same time as Jack this morning and offered him a ride down to the bus stop. He worked as an accountant for Price Waterhouse in Cherry Hill and sometimes their departures coincided.

Now he gaped at their lawn where the VIVINO FOR FREEHOLDER sign lay in tatters.

He stared a few heartbeats longer, then looked at Jack. "Was that like that when you came home last night?"

Jack shook his head. "Looked just fine when I rolled past."

Very true. Jack didn't mention that after he'd parked his bike in the garage he'd walked back and torn the sign to shreds.

He noticed something and used it to change the subject. "Hey, where's the Frisbee?"

They'd left it in the oak that grew curbside and spread over the street and the front yard. But the spot where it had lodged was empty.

"Must have fallen out during the night."

Jack scanned the front lawn. The disk was bright yellow. If there it would have been easily visible.

"Yeah, but it's not there."

His father made a sour face. "Maybe whoever tore up the sign took it." He shook his head as he gave the car some gas. "People . . . I'll never understand them. Who on earth would stop and go to the trouble to tear up Al's sign?"

Jack shrugged. "Someone who doesn't like him, I guess."

2

Jack's father accelerated away toward Cherry Hill, leaving him alone at the high school bus stop. Nobody else even in sight yet.

Southern Burlington County Regional High School—known as SBC Regional or just plain SBR for short—lay only three miles south of Johnson. Jack had wanted to ride his bike to school when the weather was decent but his folks put the kibosh on that.

His mother worried about him riding on the rutted, two-lane blacktop of Route 206. Jack had explained that he knew back roads and paths that would keep him off the highway most of the way. She hadn't bought it.

Dad's objection was that he needed the "socialization" the bus provided. Jack got the impression Dad thought he was too much of a loner and that the bus would force him to meet new kids. In other words, "socialize."

He didn't know the Connells' reasons for not wanting their kids to bike to school, but Weezy and Eddie wound up at the bus stop every morning just like Jack.

He knew of ten kids from Johnson who went to SBR. Steve Brussard, who'd been a good friend until the crazy events of last month, would have made eleven, but his mother had placed him in some private school for kids with problems. Of the ten, four of them either had cars—like Carson Toliver—or knew someone who did. The less fortunate remaining half dozen gathered by the vacant lot near the blinker light at the intersection of Quakerton

Road and 206, in front of Sumter's used car lot. The cars were still there, the little red-and-yellow pennants still fluttered on their wires, but the place had been closed since Mr. Sumter's sudden death last month. He too had been a Lodge member.

For the previous eight years Jack had waited by the vacant lot across the street for one of the grade-school buses, heading north.

The other two corners were occupied by Joe Burdett's Esso station and a Krauszer's convenience store. Jack figured the Krauszer's would come in handy for a pre-bus coffee or hot chocolate when the weather turned cold.

The lot and the shoulder were puddled from yesterday's rain. Cody Bockman posters clung to the poles supporting the blinker light over the intersection.

Gone almost forty-eight hours and still no sign of him. Jack had heard somewhere that if a crime wasn't solved in the first forty-eight hours, chances were it would never be.

So where on Earth was Cody?

Jack couldn't dodge the suspicion that the circus was somehow involved. In another day or two they'd strike their tents and be on their way to the next stop. Cody might never be found.

He glanced at the sky. Clear and sunny. No rain since yesterday afternoon. If this held up, maybe he could cut the Lodge's lawn today.

He lowered his gaze to the elementary school bus stop across the highway and saw Sally Vivino standing with her mother. Lots of mothers there this morning. Usually they took turns driving groups of the little ones down to the stop, but this morning it seemed a lot more had decided to personally see their kids off.

Trying his best to look casual, Jack crossed the road. He wanted to see how Sally was doing.

"Hi, Mrs. V," he said when he reached them. "Hi, Sally."

She stood with a Cabbage Patch Kid clutched against her chest—Jack couldn't understand the craze around those homely dolls—and looked up at him with big brown eyes.

"Hi."

No smile. Well, what could he expect?

"Hello, Jack," Mrs. Vivino said. "We haven't spoken for a long time."

Something in her voice . . . Jack couldn't read her expression because of the oversized sunglasses she wore. After seeing her bruised arms yesterday, he knew why she wore long sleeves even in warm weather like this. Was she hiding a black eye as well?

"Yeah, well . . ." The way she was staring at him made him uncomfortable. "I've wanted to stop by but . . ."

She nodded. "I understand. We missed you. Sally especially. She kept asking where you were."

Now he felt *really* bad.

"I've seen you waiting here and—"

"I've seen you too," she said. "And not just here."

What did that mean? She seemed to be trying to make a point.

"Oh?"

"I saw you last night, riding your bike away from Mr. Rosen's place."

Uh-oh.

"Yes, I, um, work for him."

She nodded, still staring at him through those dark lenses. "I know. We had a visitor yesterday. He came because of a call from a boy."

Oh, crap.

He felt himself reddening. She knew! Had she mentioned it to her husband?

Play dumb, play dumb.

"Um, a call about what?"

"About something he probably didn't understand. About something that's not his business, something he should leave alone and not get involved in."

"Oh."

He knew he was red. Had to be.

The school bus pulled up then—*in the nick of time,* as the saying went—and Jack backed away.

"Yeah, well, nice talking to you. Bye, Sally."

With a quick glance at him, Sally said, "Bye," then handed her doll to her mother and climbed on the bus.

Jack spotted Eddie and Weezy approaching the corner and hightailed it over to join them. He could feel Mrs. Vivino's gaze on his back.

3

The big yellow school bus lumbered into view and groaned to a stop. Jack was the last to board, right behind Weezy. Since Johnson was one of the later stops on the route, the bus tended to be near full by the time it reached them. Today was no exception. As usual, the older kids—the seniors without cars and the more popular juniors—had commandeered the back rows.

Only single seats remained at this point, so Weezy took one next to a girl Jack didn't know; he got waves and smiles from Karina and Cristin as he passed and wound up in a window seat next to Darren Willmon, a fellow freshman he'd met on previous trips.

Ten minutes later their bus pulled into the parking lot and stopped in line with its brothers. As he waited to get out of his seat, Jack noticed a rusty pickup pull into a far corner of the lot. Half a dozen kids of various ages jumped out of the rear bed, all wearing odd, mismatched, ill-fitting clothes.

Piney kids. He wondered if any of them were related to the trapper by the spong. Probably. Pineys were related in all sorts of ways. Some people said they were *too* closely related, like brothers and sisters getting together and having kids. Jack didn't know if any of that stuff was true. People liked to talk, and some people just naturally exaggerated as they went along. Like a game of telephone where what comes out at the end is nothing like what started it.

On the other hand, pineys weren't all that plentiful, so a piney-piney marriage could pretty much count on some sharing of family blood. The result was some kids who didn't look quite right.

He watched them troop into SBR's main building, a sprawling one-story, flat-roofed square encased in beige brick with an open central quadrangle. Whoever had designed it must have been given blueprints of Alcatraz for inspiration. All it needed was a gun tower or two to make it look like an official prison.

Inside wasn't much better: A tiled, echoey central hallway ran all around the square with classrooms left and right. A hallway branched off the southeast corner to another flat square that housed the caf. A second hall came off the southwest corner to connect to the two-story gym. The athletic field lay beyond all that.

Jack had been edgy about finding his way around when he'd started here, but he'd been a frosh for two weeks now and felt like the place was his.

4

"Next year at this time," Mr. Kressy said, pacing back and forth across the front of the classroom, "we'll be in the heat of a presidential election."

He was gray haired and overweight—not fat all over, just his belly. He looked pregnant. He always wore suspenders and a bow tie.

Jack had already chosen Mr. Kressy as his favorite teacher. He'd expected civics would be deadly dull, but Mr. Kressy made it interesting. Jack wasn't sure how he did it, but it worked. Maybe it was because he made them think rather than simply memorize.

"President Reagan will most certainly run for a second term on the Republican side. Word is that Jesse Jackson will announce that he's running for the Democratic nomination. Did anyone see the Miss America pageant on Saturday night?"

A few hands went up.

"If you did, you witnessed history of sorts: the first black woman ever to win. A black woman as Miss America, a black man running for the presidency. Times have changed, and I say it's about time. But Jesse Jackson is up against John Glenn, Walter Mondale, and a relative unknown named Gary Hart."

John Glenn—an astronaut, running for president. He'd get Jack's vote.

Smiling, Mr. Kressy paused and scanned the classroom.

"How many of you just thought, *Ooh, an astronaut! I'll vote for him*?"

A number of hands shot up, but Jack kept his down. Almost as if Mr. Kressy could read minds. And his tone hinted that John Glenn might not be such a good idea.

"Why?" Mr. Kressy said. "Because some scientists built a rocket and shot him into space? So what? The Russians did that with a monkey. Would you vote for a monkey?"

This got a laugh.

"Really: How does being an astronaut qualify him for president?"

Kelly Solt, a cute, heavyset blonde, raised her hand.

"It means he's brave."

Mr. Kressy waved an arm. "No argument there, Kelly. The monkey had no choice, but John Glenn chose to do it, and that takes courage."

Matt Follette grinned laconically from his perpetual slouch and said, "Maybe it just takes dumb."

This got a laugh. Matt had already established himself as the class cynic.

Mr. Kressy didn't seem amused. "I think we can assume he's not dumb. But the country is full of brave men—lots of ex-soldiers who risked their lives so that I could stand here and lead you in a free discussion of ideas. But that doesn't mean every one of those brave men would make a good president."

He looked around. "Anyone else?" He pointed toward the rear of the class. "Mr. Neolin . . . you look like you have something to say."

Jack turned and saw Elvin Neolin, one of the piney kids. He was small, with ruddy skin, high cheekbones, and black hair. He looked shocked that he'd been picked.

"Uuuh, no."

Bulky Jake Shuett, seated to Jack's right, leaned over and whispered, "How about that? The dumb-ass piney can talk."

Jack knew what he meant—this was the first time he'd heard the boy utter a word, but . . .

"Doesn't mean he's dumb."

Shuett made a face. "All those inbreds are retards."

Jack felt that was a pretty retarded thing to say, but let it drop. Mr. Kressy's class wasn't the place to get into it. Instead he looked at Elvin and wondered if he and his fellow pineys knew about the big pyramid on Old Man Foster's land. Maybe, maybe not. Nobody knew everything about the Barrens.

Mr. Kressy walked to the center of the room and stood a few feet from Jack.

"Okay, another show of hands. How many still want to vote for John Glenn solely because he was an astronaut?"

No hands went up this time.

"I see. I take it that means we must find other reasons to vote or not vote for him. Since the winner will be leader of the most powerful nation on Earth, maybe we should learn what the man stands for."

Karina raised her hand and said, "Don't you like what he stands for?"

"I have no idea what he stands for. At least not yet." He wandered back to the front of the room. "But he and all the others will be taking positions on certain issues. We'll hear a lot of political palaver between now and the election. I want you to listen. We have a civics book we have to study, but this is civics in action. Listen and think."

But Jack was thinking about this afternoon . . . how he was going to earn sixty bucks for mowing the Lodge's lawn while he figured out a way to get inside.

5

"You look so hot."

Jack glanced up and saw Weezy straddling her bike, shaking her head.

"As hot as Carson Toliver?"

She gave him a puzzled look, then laughed. "In your dreams."

He didn't know why he'd asked, but that wasn't an answer he liked.

She shrugged. "You know what I mean."

Yeah, he knew. And truth was, he felt *very* hot.

The grass around the Lodge was even thicker than he'd anticipated. The mower kept clogging, and the sun kept hammering away at him. After school he'd changed to a T-shirt and cut-offs before coming over, but that hadn't helped much. He was drenched.

But worth it for sixty bucks. He'd more than earn it this week, but have a much easier time next.

"Have you been able to look inside yet?"

The mower clogged and stalled again. Jack would have to unclog it, then start yanking on the cord to restart the motor. He felt his mood heading south. He gave Weezy a look.

"Boy, do you have a one-track mind. No. As you can see, I've been a little busy."

"Yeah, I guess. Still . . . every day our pyramid sits in there is like . . . a beehive buzzing in my head."

There she went again, rewriting what he'd told her. "I said I *might* have seen a pyramid."

"Only one way to find out." She shifted her gaze and stared over Jack's shoulder. "Is anybody home?"

Jack turned and realized she was looking at the Lodge.

"Whoa, Weez. We can't go snooping around here now."

"Looks empty," she said. "I wonder if the door's locked."

He could sense her getting carried away. Didn't she have any brakes on that brain of hers?

"Don't even think about it."

"Can we at least look in the windows?"

His voice rose as he felt his patience thinning. "Look, you need a little patience and I need to finish here before midnight."

"Okay, okay. When you do finish, Eddie's waiting on you to help him reach the final round of *Death Star*."

Yeah, he'd rather be handling an Atari 5200 joystick than soggy grass, rather be piloting the *Millennium Falcon* toward the Death Star's power core than pushing a mower.

"Death Star? What is a Death Star? It sounds rather entertaining."

Jack started as he looked up and saw Mr. Drexler, wearing his ever-present white suit, standing in the Lodge's front entrance beneath the huge sigil.

How long had he been there? Had he heard anything?

"It's in a movie," Jack said. "Science fiction."

His interest vaporized. "Oh. I don't like fiction."

Weezy looked jumpy. Jack understood. Even though the Lodge had been here forever, probably before the town, maybe before the Pilgrims—long before the Indians, according to her—it was fanatically secretive and mysterious and nobody knew what to make of it. And here she'd been talking about poking around inside it.

Giving her a keep-mum look, he left her behind and

walked over to Mr. Drexler. Mainly because he was standing in the shade, but also because Jack wanted to broach a certain topic. He hesitated, then decided to go for it.

"What's it like inside?" Jack said, pointing to the building.

Mr. Drexler regarded him. "It is what one might call 'functional.'"

"Do you give tours?"

"Tours?" he said, his eyebrows lifting. "Tours are only for prospective members during recruitment. You are too young for recruitment."

"But you recruited my father and gave him a tour."

"Then you can ask him all about it."

"He won't tell me much. How about it? Make an exception for the son of a recruit who turned you down?"

"That's hardly reason for an exception." He sighed. "I might give you a cursory tour sometime, but not today."

Yes!

"Can I bring a friend?"

Mr. Drexler nodded toward where Weezy waited with her bike. "By 'friend' I suppose you mean your girlfriend, the contentious Miss Connell."

"She's not my girlfriend." Though she could be contentious as all get-out. "But yeah."

"I would hope she wouldn't think she was going to find her precious missing artifact inside."

"Who, Weezy? Not a chance. So how about it?"

"I suppose."

Yes!

As Mr. Drexler turned away and closed the door, Jack hurried back to where Weezy waited.

"We're going on a tour of the Lodge," he whispered.

Her eyes nearly bugged out of their sockets. "Ohmygod, I can't believe it. When?"

"Not sure yet, but I'll bug him till he gives in. Operation Pyramid is *on!*"

6

"I'm going out for a little bit," Jack said.

Dinner was over and he was feeling restless. His father looked up from where he sat sipping an after-dinner beer with Mr. Bainbridge, a fellow Korean War vet.

"Okay, Jack. Homework done?"

He shrugged. "Yeah. Just going for a ride."

"Don't be too long." He raised a hand. "Oh, Mom says you're cutting the Lodge's lawn?"

"Those nuts?" Mr. Bainbridge said.

Jack nodded. "Mister Drexler's paying me sixty bucks."

Dad's eyebrows shot up. "Sixty!" Then his eyes narrowed. "He just came out and offered you sixty bucks?"

"No. It was less at first but—"

"You negotiated more?"

"Well . . ." Jack couldn't really call it negotiating. He'd hesitated and Mr. Drexler had interpreted that as dissatisfaction with the initial offer of fifty.

Dad smiled. "Good for you."

Mr. Bainbridge laughed and slapped his thigh. "Damn, Jack! Maybe I should take you with me next time I buy a car!"

Outside, Jack looked around his front yard. Too dark to see anything now. He'd scoured the whole area this afternoon, looking for that Frisbee. The bushes, the street, the neighbors' yards—not a sign of it. All he could think of was some dog had come along and run off with it.

He hopped on his bike and accelerated. Yeah, he was off

on a ride, but he had a destination in mind: the Vivino house.

He'd thought about Sally while he was mowing the Lodge's lawn, during dinner, and through his homework. He knew it was crazy, but he had to go check on her.

Dusk was fading to night as he cut past the Bainbridge house on his way to the highway. He spotted a dark figure rocking on the front porch. Weird Walt, no doubt. His sister was married to Mr. Bainbridge and he lived with them.

Down on Quakerton he passed USED. All looked quiet there. He hadn't given a thought to opening it today because Mr. Rosen always kept it closed on Mondays.

He rode up 206 to Mr. Rosen's place and leaned his bike against the side of the trailer. Then he crept into the Vivino yard and up to the house. His heart jumped, then sank when he heard Sally screaming.

He stole to the side of the house and followed the sound to one of the kitchen windows. He suppressed a gasp when he peeked in and saw Mr. Vivino holding his wife in an armlock. Her expression looked agonized but she wasn't saying anything. Her husband seemed to be doing all the talking but Jack couldn't hear what he was saying over Sally's screams.

"Stop it, Daddy! Stop-it-stop-it-stop-it!"

Unable to watch, Jack reeled away from the window and ran back to his bike. When he reached it he stood panting—not from exertion, from rage.

This couldn't go on. Mr. Vivino had to be stopped. But that didn't seem doable unless Mrs. V stopped covering for him.

Had to be another way. Had to be.

As he rolled his bike back toward the highway, he saw the

lights from the circus up the road. He rode up there, looking for distraction, but when he reached the entrance he found he had no interest in wandering the midway again.

So he turned around and headed slowly back to town. A fog was rolling in so he switched sides and rode against the traffic to see what was coming, all the while cudgeling his brain for a solution. He considered talking to his dad about it. But what could he do? Go up to Mr. Vivino and say, *My son's been spying on your family and says you've been mistreating Cathy and Sally.*

Like that would do a lot of good—especially if Mrs. V said nothing was wrong.

Everything seemed to hinge on her.

Or maybe he should just mind his own damn business. Yeah, that was exactly what he should do.

But he knew he couldn't.

7

Jack pedaled through the foggy town, still unable to think of a solution. Instead of turning off on North Franklin, he followed Quakerton Road toward the lake to see how it looked in the fog.

Well, it looked like . . . fog, and nothing but fog; the mist had grown impenetrably thick over the surface, masking the lake and its shores. The fully lit Lodge seemed to float above it, like a boxy cruise ship. He'd never seen it so lit up, so he crossed into Old Town for a closer look. He found perhaps a dozen cars parked around it.

Well, well, well. Was the Septimus Order throwing a party?

An unbidden image of Mr. Drexler dancing around with a lampshade on his head made Jack cringe.

Curious, he leaned his bike against the curb and wandered across the lawn. The cars parked on the gravel driveway were of all types, ranging from limousines to pickups. About a dozen feet from the building, he paused. He really shouldn't be here. If he got caught he'd probably lose the lawn job and the sixty bucks a week that went with it, plus the chance at a tour of the place.

Nope, not worth the risk.

With an effort he turned and was starting back toward his bike when he heard a faint, high-pitched cry—like a child's voice. He froze and waited, listening. He heard the breeze whispering through the pines and rustling the leaves of the maples that lined the street, but no—

There. Again. The high-pitched cry.

Cody? Could it be . . . ?

He did a slow turn, trying to identify the direction it had come from. The fog diffused the sound, making it seem to come from everywhere at once. The only place near enough for a source was the Lodge.

Jack headed back toward the building. He didn't see any choice but to take a look. If Cody was in there . . .

He didn't want to think about it.

Lowering to a crouch, he eased up to one of the front windows and peered between the bars into a room with a huge fireplace. No one in sight, and the spot where he thought he'd seen the pyramid wasn't visible from this angle.

He heard the cry again. It seemed to come from around the corner.

Staying low, he slipped along the stucco wall toward the rear of the building. There he peeked into another large room, this one crowded with men gathered around a large table. The familiar sigil of the Ancient Septimus Fraternal Order was painted on the ceiling, looking down on the table like a watchful alien eye. Some of the men wore suits, some dressed more casually, but all were avidly staring at something on the table. Jack couldn't see what it was because they blocked his view.

His gut twisted as he imagined them torturing Cody in some foul secret rite. And then someone stepped away, leaving a gap that revealed what was so interesting. Jack recognized it immediately.

The Mystery Machine from the circus sideshow.

And now he spotted its owner, the thin man the canvas boss had called "Prather." Mr. Prather appeared to be explaining something about the gizmo to the Lodge members, and they all seemed fascinated. Then the man who'd moved away stepped back, blocking Jack's view again.

He backed away from the window. More evidence of a connection between the Order and the Taber & Sons circus. But so what? It didn't mean anything unless the circus was involved with Cody's disappearance.

And if that cry hadn't come from Cody, then who—?

Jack jumped as a sound broke the silence from directly to his left, louder and higher pitched than the previous cries. He looked and saw nothing at first, then a pair of eyes flashed as they caught the light from the window.

A cat . . . a fat tabby looked up at him and made that sound again. From farther away, through the fog, Jack imagined it could have sounded like a frightened child. He chased it away and stood listening.

All quiet.

He gave up and headed back to his bike.

8

Mr. Bainbridge was leaving just as Jack got home. He could tell from his eyes he'd had more than a couple of Dad's Carling Black Labels.

"Gonna make it to the smoker on Thursday?" Mr. Bainbridge asked his father.

Jack knew that "the smoker" was the monthly get-together at the VFW post where they drank, played cards, and showed porno movies.

Dad shook his head. "Not my cup of tea, Kurt. You know that."

"Yeah, but we finally got rid of those old eight-millimeters. We've got a VCR now and we can rent all sorts of new stuff." He laughed. "All in living color!"

Dad gave him a tolerant smile and waved. "You boys have fun."

Mom walked in as he left. She held a dish towel. "That was Kate on the phone. She was talking to Tim and he says they're stalled on Cody. The state police are involved now. They had a search party in the Pines today and they're planning on going back tomorrow. They dragged the lake and found nothing. They're also searching the cornfields and the orchards. There's so many places he could be." She twisted the towel and looked about to cry. "His poor parents. Think what they must be going through."

"He's got to be somewhere."

As soon as the words left his mouth Jack wanted to kick himself for saying something so ridiculously obvious. Of course Cody was somewhere. Everybody was somewhere. Question was: Wherever he was, was he alive?

It seemed less and less likely to Jack that this was going to have a happy ending.

9

That night Jack dreamed he was at the Taber & Sons circus, showing off for Karina at the ring-the-bell game. Tony Vivino was nowhere in sight this time, but his mother and Sally were, and he wondered why until he realized that Mr. Vivino's head had replaced the ringer weight. He swung the mallet in a mighty arc that sent Mr. V's head to the top and rang the bell. The instant-home-movie guy from the bumper cars was taping it all and everyone was having a great time until Cody Bockman showed up with Mr. Prather's Mystery Machine and dissolved everyone with the disintegrating ray it created.

1

After Mr. Kressy's class, Karina went through the caf line with Jack and they joined a table with Eddie and a few other kids. As he pulled up a chair Jack noticed Elvin Neolin approaching. They made brief eye contact and Jack started to wave him over. He didn't know any of the pineys and Elvin seemed like an okay guy. Shy as all get-out, but maybe Jack could draw him out . . . see if he knew anything about a pyramid in the Pines.

But Jake Shuett raised a hand in a stop signal. "Don't even think about it, piney. We don't eat with inbreds."

Elvin's gaze dropped and he veered away.

Karina slammed her hands on the table. "*What?*"

Matt Follette and Erik Burns looked up from their food and Eddie stopped fiddling with his Rubik's Cube.

Jake looked surprised. "Hey—"

Karina jabbed a finger at his face from across the table. "Don't you *ever* say 'we' when I'm around. I'm not part of you, I'm not like you, and I don't want to be included with you."

She began putting her food back onto her tray.

Jack watched Elvin approach another table occupied by fellow pineys, then turned to Jake.

"That was pretty cold, Shuett. And you don't speak for me either."

"What is it with you two?" Jake said. "He's a piney. They're retards. He's probably going to marry his sister just like his daddy did."

Karina's eyes blazed. "Mostly they're just poor. Some don't have electricity or running water, but that brother-sister stuff is garbage."

"What did you say to Elvin?" said a new voice.

Jack looked up and saw a tall skinny kid with long, unruly brown hair. His clothes were too small, leaving his gangly arms sticking out of his sleeves and his cuffs above his ankles. He had one blue eye and one brown. His mismatched gaze was fixed on Jake.

Jake seemed to shrink for an instant, then he puffed up. He had ten or fifteen pounds on the new kid. He picked up a ketchup pack and casually began shaking it down.

"Who wants to know?"

"My name's Levi Coffin."

Jake snickered. "Coffin? Is that a made-up name like Sid Vicious?"

He looked around the table. If he was expecting a laugh, he was disappointed. Jack was feeling acutely uncomfortable.

"It's an old Quaker name," Levi said. "And I'm asking if you called El an inbred."

Jake tried to stare him down. "Yeah. I did. What're you going to do about it?"

The guy didn't flinch. "Just wanted to make sure."

With that he turned and walked away.

Jack wondered if a threat had been issued.

Jake's laugh sounded forced. "Another piney loser."

Just then his ketchup pack exploded, spraying his shirtfront with crimson sauce.

As he cursed and grabbed for a paper napkin, he must have knocked against his plate, because it spilled his burger and cole slaw onto his lap.

Everyone at the table burst out laughing as he jumped from his seat and danced around, wiping himself off.

"Man, I don't believe this!"

Karina grinned as she picked up her tray and stepped away from the table.

"Talk about an inbred retard!"

Jake reddened. He looked like he wanted to say something but couldn't think of anything. He hurried from the caf, probably headed for the boys' room.

Karina sat down again. "Well, if he's leaving, I'll stay."

Jack leaned back and looked at her, then at Levi Coffin, reseating himself with the other pineys, then at the retreating Jake Shuett.

What a weird chain of events. He had the strangest feeling that something had happened here, something more than what he'd seen. But what?

He shrugged it off and looked at Karina. She was something else.

He gave her a smile. "Next time, don't hold back—tell Jake how you really feel."

Her returning smile was warm as she looked him in the eye. "Sometimes keeping quiet is just like agreeing. Thanks for backing me up."

Karina struck him as a thinker, like Weezy. He liked that. And she'd even been in his dream last night—

The dream—it fast-forwarded through his head. No way he could tell her he'd been dreaming about her—especially not in front of this crew. Be cool if he could somehow get hold of the videotape that circus guy had been recording in the dream. He could show Karina. Then again, it had been so weird it might scare her off.

He stiffened.

Videotape . . .

. . . show the videotape.

"Jack?" Karina said. "Something wrong?"

"Hmmm? No. Just had an idea."

A very cool idea about something that waited—he hoped—at USED. He prayed Mr. Rosen hadn't sold it.

2

School seemed to drag for an eternity. As soon as Jack got home he grabbed the keys to USED and raced to the store.

As long as I'm here, he thought as he unlocked the front door, might as well open for business.

He shut the door and flipped the CLOSED sign to OPEN. Then he headed straight for the rear of the store.

Where was it? Where had he put it?

There—he recognized the gray carrying case. He pulled it out and unzipped it to reveal a video camera. Mr. Rosen had bought it off a guy last month. Expecting a quick turnover, he'd put it in the window, but no one had seemed interested. Eventually he'd had Jack move it back into the store to make room for something else in the scarce window space.

Lucky for me, Jack thought.

Because he had a use for it.

He thumbed through the manual, found the charger in a side pocket of the case, and plugged it into the wall. He planned to study the manual during the charging period, but the bell above the front door jangled.

A customer?

He walked forward and recognized Mark Mulliner. Jack assumed the woman carrying the baby behind him was his wife.

"Hey," Mark said with an easy smile. "Got any screwdrivers? Dropped mine in the lake."

Jack glanced out the window and saw a pickup with canoes piled in the bed. Mark rented them out at the lake during the summer.

"End of the season for the canoes?" he said as he pulled a plastic bucket full of old tools from under a shelf and set it on the counter.

Mark started sorting through the screwdrivers and pliers and such.

"Yeah. Temperature's right but the rain's a killer."

Jack glanced at the dark-haired baby girl. He waved and she smiled, showing a couple of brand-new teeth.

"Say hello, Poppy," said her mom.

"Here we go," Mark said, holding up a long flat-head screwdriver. "This'll do."

He paid for it and they left just as Weird Walt came in.

"Hey, Jack. I thought Mister Rosen said he was gonna be in New York this week."

He leaned on the counter, close enough so Jack could smell the applejack on his breath. The number of people who'd seen Walt completely sober was about the same as those who'd seen him without gloves.

Jack explained that he'd promised to open the store now and then while Mr. Rosen was away.

"That's cool. Hey, whatta y'think about finding that bike?"

"What bike?"

"The little kid's—Cody Bockman's."

Jack's neck tensed. "They found it? Where?"

"Not too far into the Pines, on Old Man Foster's land."

He didn't know if he wanted an answer to his next question.

"They find anything else?"

Walt shook his head. "Nah. But the sheriff's organizing a

big search party tomorrow morning. Everybody fourteen and up who wants to join is supposed to gather at the lightning tree at oh-eight-hundred, rain or shine."

"But shouldn't we be worrying about the equinox?" Jack said, remembering the warning Walt had given him the other day.

Walt looked confused for a few seconds, then the light dawned. "Oh, yeah. But this'll be a big group, and it's during the day. The real equinox ain't due till after sundown."

"Okay, then," Jack said. "Count me in. No, wait—I've got school."

"Sheriff says any kid who joins the search is excused from school."

Jack raised a fist. "I'm there."

But that was tomorrow. He had something important he had to do tonight.

3

"Subcontracting?"

Jack, squatting as he weeded the foundation beds on the Lodge's north flank, looked up to see Mr. Drexler, again all in white—didn't he own any other color? Weezy squatted beside him, helping.

It had rained again last night, but that didn't interfere with weeding. They each used a short spade to dig under the weeds and help pull them out by their roots. They'd shake off the excess soil, toss them into a plastic bag, smooth out the mulch, and move to the next.

"I'm a volunteer," Weezy said with a pasted-on smile and a sticky-sweet tone.

She was helping solely as an excuse to hang around the Lodge in case the tour materialized. Jack knew the effort it took her to make nice-nice with someone from the Order, but he'd warned her that mouthing off could queer everything.

"Really? Why would one volunteer for such hot, dirty, menial labor?"

The smile remained. "It's what friends do."

"I'd think a true friend would pay you at least minimum wage."

"Oh my," she said, cocking her head and sounding like Glinda the Good Witch of the North, "friends don't take money from friends."

Jack didn't know how long she could keep up the façade, so he jumped to what mattered most.

"Are we getting our tour today?"

Mr. Drexler frowned. "Tour? Whatever are you talking about?"

Jack looked at Weezy and saw her eyes narrowing.

"Yesterday you said you'd give us a tour of the Lodge."

"I believe I said 'might.' But I continue to have doubts about including Miss Connell. I don't want to worry about her opening cabinets and drawers in search of her lost artifact."

Jack gave her a be-cool look as he said, "Oh, that won't be a problem. Right, Weez?"

He sent up a silent prayer that she'd be able to play along. If this tour meant anything to her, she'd rein in the emotions that tended to run wild where the pyramid was concerned.

But she surprised him by staying perfectly cool—at least on the outside.

"I wouldn't think of it, Mister Drexler. I promise to keep my hands in my pockets. You can even handcuff me if you want."

He shook his head and turned away. "I'm having serious second thoughts about this. I'm rescinding my offer."

Weezy's eyes ignited and her lips pulled back, baring her teeth as she started to rise to her feet. Jack pulled her back with a warning look. He was just as surprised, disappointed, and angry, but all might not yet be lost. If she detonated, however . . .

Mr. Drexler turned back just as suddenly as he'd turned away.

"By the way, I understand you discovered the artifact within a box. Was it locked?"

Weezy had her head down, stabbing her little spade into the dirt like an Aztec priestess cutting out a heart.

"No," Jack said, "just hard to open."

He leaned forward. "Who opened it?"

"Me."

The blue eyes narrowed. "Really. How interesting."

"Yeah. Seemed I was the only one who could. Oh, yeah, and Mister Brussard could too. But he's, you know . . ."

"Yes. The late Brother Brussard . . ." He stared at Jack for what seemed like a long time, then motioned to him and Weezy. "Follow me now if you wish that tour."

Mr. Drexler moved toward the rear of the Lodge. Baffled, Jack glanced at a very shocked-looking Weezy. But the shock turned to wild anticipation as she sprang to her feet and started after him. Jack held her back a second.

"Remember," he whispered. "I only thought I saw the pyramid. If we don't see it inside, stay cool."

She nodded and followed Mr. Drexler. Jack brought up the rear, wondering what had made him change his mind.

He led them through the rear door that opened into some sort of mud room.

"Only members are allowed entrance through the front."

"Why is that?" Jack said.

"Because that is the way it has always been." He gestured to the next room, a small kitchen with a stove and a fridge, but old-fashioned. "Antiquated, yes. A holdover from the days when the Lodge had residents. Eggers and I have used it on occasion, but it is by and large a vestigial space."

They moved through a short hallway into a large room dominated by a long table flanked with leather chairs. The sigil on the ceiling confirmed it as the crowded room he'd peeked in on last night.

Weezy seemed to have lost her voice, but her wide eyes

never stopped moving as her gaze lasered into every nook and cranny.

"This is the conference room, where the members meet to discuss matters of concern to the Order and themselves."

Light through the barred windows reflected off the table's smeared, dusty surface.

Messy, Jack thought.

He'd have figured a dapper guy like Mr. Drexler to be a neatnik.

As if reading Jack's thoughts, the man said, "The premises need a thorough cleaning. I don't wish to be bothered with anyone here during my stay, but a crew will be through as soon as I depart."

"Really?"

Mr. Drexler looked at him. "You're surprised that we'd want to keep the place clean?"

"No . . . just surprised you let anyone in."

"The cleaning service is owned by a brother, and the workers will be personally supervised by him."

Jack noticed the paintings lining the walls. Weezy stopped before the portrait of a stern-looking man in medieval clothing.

She found her voice. "Who's that?"

"A former Arch of the worldwide High Council of the Seven."

Jack repressed a laugh. "Well, that clears that up."

Mr. Drexler allowed one of his tight smiles. "Briefly: The Order is ruled by the High Council of the Seven, and the leading member of the Council is known as the Arch. All the men you see here are former Arches. The portraits are not originals, of course. They are copies of archived paintings."

Jack checked them out, one after the other.

"So all these guys—" she said.

"Arches, please. Show some respect."

"Sorry. All these 'Arches' knew the Secret History of the World?"

Mr. Drexler gave her an appraising look. "Do you really think such a history exists?"

She looked him square in the eye. "Absolutely."

She'd often told Jack that the Septimus Order was guardian of certain truths that had been kept secret and passed on throughout the history of the world, and that knowledge of those truths allowed them to manipulate people and events—history itself.

Mr. Drexler's lips twisted. "Perhaps you are right, but you will never find out."

"Why not?"

"Because women are not allowed in the Order." He turned to Jack. "But you can learn, should you ever be asked to join."

"And accept."

The man frowned. "Don't make your father's mistake and turn down the invitation. It is offered only once. Who knows how far he could have gone?" He gestured to the portraits. "He could have been here among the Movers." He turned and pointed to one of the windows. "Instead he's out there with the Moved. Such a shame."

Jack had no idea what he was talking about, but couldn't help smile. "Believe it or not, he seems to be bearing up pretty well."

"Only because he doesn't know what he is missing."

Jack noticed other paintings interspersed among the portraits, mostly of buildings.

"What are these?"

"Other Lodges. The Septimus Order is global."

Jack heard Weezy gasp as she stopped before a painting. "Look!"

Jack stepped over to see and suppressed a gasp of his own. She was staring at a painting of the pyramid cage in the woods, but this had no broken section. The faces of its megaliths were clean and smooth, and the glyphs carved into each were clearly visible—the same as on their little pyramid. It sat in a landscaped clearing under a sunny sky. The trees around it looked more like palms than pines.

"Is that a Lodge too?" Jack said, knowing it wasn't.

Drexler came up behind them. "Oh, no. That is simply an ancient decorative structure."

"Decorative?" Weezy pointed to a dark shape in the shadows within. "Then what's that in there?"

"You'd have to ask the artist, and I'm afraid he's long dead. Now come this way."

Jack looked at Weezy and found her staring back. They both looked again at the painting. No question about it: The artist had painted something trapped in that cage. Something big.

The painting was one more connection between the Lodge and the pyramids—big and little.

Now . . . find the little one—*if* it was here.

They followed Mr. Drexler into a large sitting room, the one Jack had peeked at through the front entrance. It was furnished with comfy-looking, overstuffed chairs. A rug woven with the sigil design covered most of the hardwood floor, and another sigil overhung a jumbo fireplace shielded by a brass fire screen decorated with—surprise—another sigil.

"This room is for less formal gatherings," Mr. Drexler said.

Jack barely heard him. His attention immediately fixed

on the high mantel where he'd glimpsed the little black object, but now he saw no sign of it.

Weezy was staring too, a dismayed look on her face.

Had he imagined it, or had Mr. Drexler removed it before letting them in?

Motioning Weezy to stay in the center of the room, he wandered in that direction.

"Wow. Neat fireplace."

Nothing the least bit special about it—he simply wanted a closer look at the mantel.

"It is still used on rare occasions," he heard Mr. Drexler say behind him.

Jack made a show of peeking behind the fire screen. He checked out the large brass andirons, then straightened and stretched up onto his toes for a quick close look at the mantel. There, front and center on its dusty surface, was a small hexagon of clean wood.

Six sides, just like their little pyramid.

Gotcha-gotcha-gotcha!

It took all Jack's will not to call Weezy over and show her, but he didn't want to risk an explosion.

He could think of only one reason they'd remove it before his tour: It was the same pyramid he and Weezy had found in the mound. The fact that the Order had been able to steal it from where they had testified to the group's long reach.

Maybe it had been theirs to begin with. Maybe it had been stolen and, for some reason known only to members of the Order, buried along with the murdered man Jack and Weezy had found.

If it had been the Order's originally, fine. Say so and

claim it. But they'd said nothing. Why not? Afraid to draw attention to their oh-so-secret Lodge? Whatever the reason, they'd chosen instead to steal it from Weezy and Jack.

Well, because the Order had never claimed it, as far as Jack was concerned, finders keepers. It belonged to Weezy and him.

And he wanted it back.

But how to get it?

Well, it had been stolen from him, so he guessed it would be only right for him to steal it back.

He'd composed himself by the time he turned to face Mr. Drexler again. Weezy was staring at him, the question writ large on her face. He gave away nothing.

"Really cool," he said. "What's upstairs?"

"We won't be going there. It is divided into smaller rooms, leftover from the day when the Lodge had residents. Eggers and I are using two of those now, but there's nothing of interest there. Same with the basement: used simply for storage."

Jack wandered over to the front door. From past experience he knew it was steel, but he hadn't realized that the lock was a double-key dead bolt. The key sat in the inner keyhole now.

"I, um, thought you'd have an alarm system."

Mr. Drexler's eyebrows lifted. "Why would you think that?"

"Well, the place is empty all the time—I mean, until you showed up. Someone could come in and rob you."

He gave his sort-of smile. "It might prove rather entertaining if someone tried."

"No, really."

"Rob us of what? There's nothing of value here except

the furniture. And to take that they'd have to back a van up to the front door. We have bars on the windows and locks on the doors. Quite enough, I think."

Jack nodded. "Yeah, I guess so."

The first-floor windows were all barred, but even though the ones on the second floor were not, he couldn't imagine any way to reach them short of a ladder.

Mr. Drexler clapped his hands once. "End of tour. I hope your curiosity is satisfied."

Weezy's expression became stony. "I'd really like to see the rest of the place."

"Sorry. Not included."

Jack gave her another be-cool look. He saw her take a deep breath and set her lips in a thin line. But as they passed between the front room and the rear conference room, she froze.

"Did you hear that?"

"Hear what?" Jack hadn't heard a thing.

"It sounded like a child."

Jack's skin tingled. He almost said he'd heard something like that right outside last night, but held back. He wasn't supposed to have been right outside last night.

A heavy, dark oak door stood closed to her right. She pulled it open, revealing a stairway down to a dark basement.

"What is this, now? I thought we agreed you would confine yourself to what I showed you."

"But I heard—"

"You heard nothing. You are merely looking for an excuse to hunt for your imaginary artifact."

Weezy stood at the top of the stairs, eyes closed, listening. But whatever sound she was waiting for never came.

Mr. Drexler pushed the door closed and gestured toward the rear of the Lodge.

"Thanks for the tour," Jack said as they reached the back door.

Weezy said nothing.

On the way out he noticed the rear door was steel too, with a double-key dead bolt to boot. He figured he might be able to pick it, but man, oh, man . . .

Sure. Easy enough to say he'd steal it back, but if he got caught he was certain the Lodge would use all its many connections in high places to make sure he was prosecuted to the max.

Breaking in here . . . an awfully big step. Risky. He'd be crazy to try.

Had to be another way.

4

"I *know* I heard something," Weezy said as they walked across the lawn.

Jack told her about what he'd heard last night.

"A cat?" she said when he finished. "That didn't sound like any cat to me."

"I didn't hear it, so I can't say. And you didn't hear it again."

She sighed. "No. I guess it could have been something else."

He waited until they'd reached the curb before saying, "Maybe it was the pyramid crying out to you—because they've got it."

Her eyes widened. "You're sure?"

"What do you think: The mantel is dusty but there's a hexagon of clean wood right where I saw something black and pointy."

She spun and started toward the Lodge. "I'm going back!"

He grabbed her arm. "And do what? He won't let you in. Probably won't even answer the door. Let's not tip our hand."

"We've got to find a way in there!"

"Easier said than done. He hardly ever goes out, and even if he does, the place is locked up like Fort Knox."

"We'll think of something. And we'll do it together." She put out her hand. "Deal?"

"Deal."

They shook.

"And while we're thinking," she said, "maybe we should take another look at the big pyramid—for inspiration."

"You think it's the same one in the painting?"

"I'd bet my copy of the Secret History of the World."

"But you don't—"

"If I did, I would."

"And what do we hope to find there? Another little pyramid?"

Her dark eyes sparkled. "That'd be nice. No, I'm thinking we might find evidence of whatever was kept in there—maybe remains of the thing itself. Another piece of the Secret History. Wouldn't that be something?"

"It would," Jack said, looking back at the Lodge, "but I've got to finish up the weeds and trim all the bushes by tomorrow afternoon."

"Why then?"

"He won't say so, but I think it has something to do with the equinox."

Weezy glanced toward Mrs. Clevenger's place up the street. "Did you get the warning?"

"About staying out of the Pines? Yeah, Walt told me all sorts of weird things can happen in there. What do you think?"

Weezy smiled. "I think we're obligated to check it out."

"I thought you'd say that."

"We're on?"

"Of course. I'm not letting you have all the fun."

Jack felt a little uneasy about ignoring Mrs. C's warning, but he couldn't back out and leave Weezy to go on her own.

But really . . . they knew the woods. What could happen?

5

I must be crazy, Jack thought as he slipped along the hedge separating Mr. Rosen's yard from the Vivinos'.

After dinner, he'd picked up the video camera at USED, then ridden out here. His bike now was leaning against the far side of Mr. Rosen's trailer and the camera hung by its strap from his shoulder.

He found a spot behind a big spirea. Its dense tangle of fine branches offered good cover. It sat within earshot of the house, so he settled down to wait.

Alarms kept ringing in his brain, warning him about how much trouble he'd be in if he ever got caught. He knew they were right but he ignored them. He had to. He'd committed himself to this. For Sally and her mother.

Save them, Jack. I can't do it, so you've gotta. Save them.

Yeah, and for Tony too.

A spotlight from the house shone on the pool area. The gate on the chain-link fence was closed. A pink beach ball sat between a pair of lounge chairs.

In the house, all quiet except for voices from the TV filtering through the window screens. He tried to identify the show but couldn't.

He'd skimmed through the camera manual and reviewed what he'd read. Not much to operating the thing: turn it on, sight through the viewfinder, and press the little red REC button.

He felt torn as he sat and listened. Part of him hoped for peace and quiet in the Vivino household tonight, and another knew that if he didn't expose the mistreatment, it would go on and on.

But how to expose it? Assuming he did capture something damning on the tape, what to do with it? Send it to a newspaper?

Nah. That wouldn't work. They'd probably give it to the police, and without Mrs. V's cooperation he'd be back to square one.

He had a brief fantasy about sneaking into the cable-TV company's studio and running it on the local access channel. Hardly anybody watched it, but enough would see the tape to start talking about it, spread the word about what was going on in the Vivino house, and pretty soon everyone would know. And if everyone knew, Mr. Vivino would have to change his ways.

But that was a no go. Even if Jack could sneak into the studio or the control booth, he wouldn't know how to put the tape on air.

The Freeholders? Maybe send the tape to the Board of Freeholders and let them know what they were allowing into their midst. But was that enough?

Jack decided to shelve it for now. First he had to capture something. If he didn't do that, the other questions didn't matter.

As he waited in silence, he noticed a flicker of light near the western horizon.

Lightning?

The sky was clear except for clouds to the far west, and the moon hadn't risen yet. The murky glitter of the Milky Way arched overhead. Didn't look like rain, but he hadn't listened for the weather before going out, so he didn't—

Another flicker. No question—lightning. Another storm on the way. Weren't they ever going to stop?

He thought he saw movement in the front yard, beyond the glow from the lit windows. He squinted through the darkness but didn't see anything out of place or that shouldn't be there.

Then he caught the stench.

He knew that stink. The hulking shadow they'd seen in the Pines last month had smelled just like this. The odor seemed to be all around him, like an invisible cloud. He couldn't tell where it was coming from, because the air was so still. That meant it could be close. Very close.

Then Mr. Vivino's voice broke the silence. "What on God's Earth is *that*? What's that smell?"

The stench must have drifted inside. The front door opened then and Mr. Vivino stepped out on his steps and looked around.

"God! Did something die out here?"

"Is it a skunk?" Mrs. V called from inside.

"No. I've smelled skunk and this is no skunk."

Jack shrank back as the man came down the steps and began walking around his yard.

Don't come over here!

But he did just that.

As Mr. Vivino approached, Jack looked frantically about for an escape route but had none. Couldn't go through the hedge—too much noise. Couldn't run—no cover. No choice but to stay put.

So he crouched in the deep shadow at the base of the bush and wished he had a hole to duck into. He tried to make himself as small as possible, curling into a tight fetal position with his forehead down against his knees. The starshine didn't offer much light and Mr. Vivino had just come from indoors. His eyes wouldn't be adjusted yet.

Jack tensed as he heard footsteps approach. His bladder wanted to empty. If Mr. Vivino found him here, no telling what he'd do. He outweighed Jack by an easy hundred pounds. If he lost that temper of his . . .

But worse than a beating would be what would come after: caught with a camera outside someone's home. Everyone would think he was a Peeping Tom, he'd be labeled a perv—

The footsteps stopped on the other side of the bush, not two feet away. Jack held his breath and watched the shoes turn this way and that.

He heard Mr. Vivino sniffing the air. The odor had faded.

"I'll be damned," he muttered.

"Did you find anything?" Mrs. V said from a second-floor window.

"No, not a thing. Maybe just a cloud of stink passing through from the highway."

"Do you think it was dangerous? I mean, toxic?"

"Nah. Didn't smell chemical, it just smelled . . . *ripe*."

Ripe . . . perfect word for it, Jack thought. Now turn around and go back inside.

After a couple of seconds, Mr. Vivino did just that.

But Jack didn't move. Even after he heard the front door slam he remained curled up.

And while he hid there he thought about the exchange he had just heard between Mr. and Mrs. Vivino. They'd sounded so normal, so much like a regular couple that Jack wondered if he'd imagined the violence he'd seen.

No, he hadn't imagined anything.

So . . . could that be the way they were? He gets mad and beats on her and whacks and yells at Sally, and then in the times between they're just Mr. and Mrs. Average American Family?

Very strange.

But whatever, he'd had enough tonight. More than enough.

The rumble of thunder in the distance only underscored his need to be gone from this place.

He uncoiled slowly and sniffed. No stench. He checked the front yard: all clear. Same with the back—

He took a second look. Hadn't he seen a pink beach ball between the two lounge chairs before? No biggie. A breeze probably rolled it away.

He squeezed through the hedge into Mr. Rosen's yard, found his bike and headed toward the safety and sanity of his own home.

And it *was* pretty sane, wasn't it. Talk about the Average American Family. He had a rock-steady father who worked hard but always made time for him, a stay-at-home mother who volunteered at the hospital and called him her "miracle boy"—and though he hated the term, he recognized the love behind it. Two parents who hardly ever argued—or if they did, kept it out of earshot.

He would have liked to live in a bigger town, one with at least a movie theater and a McDonald's within bike distance. But on the upside, Johnson was a town with no crime, where most folks never locked their doors.

They weren't rich and he didn't have everything he wanted—like a rifle—but he didn't lack for anything meaningful, including a great sister. The only fly in the ointment was his jerk brother, but nothing was perfect. And Tom was away at law school, which made him almost bearable. Whatever family bumps Jack had encountered along the way had been minor—certainly nothing like a death or even a serious illness to contend with.

He felt like he lived in a peaceful bubble. He wondered if it would ever pop.

Never, he hoped.

WEDNESDAY

1

Jack, Weezy, and Eddie walked through Old Town toward the lightning tree.

After more rain last night, the lake was way past its banks now. It would be leaking onto the streets soon, and then into people's basements. Because Old Town sat uphill from the lake, the water would flow west. Jack's house was blocks away, but who knew where and how fast the water would flow once it hit the streets?

"Something's got to be done about this," he heard his mother say.

She, along with Mrs. Connell and a few other ladies from town, was walking behind them, all headed to volunteer in the big Cody Bockman search.

"We should talk to the Freeholders about pumping it out," Weezy's mom said.

Pumping it *where*? Jack thought. Into the Pines? That's going to take a monster pump and one long, long hose.

One thing was certain: If it kept raining, someone was going to have to do something.

Lots of cars were parked up and down Quakerton Road. The locals were turning out in big numbers. After crossing the bridge and walking through Old Town, he was pleasantly surprised to see a couple of hundred people of all ages gathered around the police cars near the barkless, burned-out trunk of the lightning tree.

He saw Walt and his sister, Mrs. Bainbridge, Jeff Colton from Burdett's Esso station, Mrs. Courtland, one of his lawn-mowing customers, plus Professor Nakamura and his wife.

He glanced at Weezy and saw her glaring at the professor. They'd left the pyramid in his care to be examined by experts, and had never seen it again.

"Come on, Weez," he said in a low voice. "I know you're ticked at him, but let's keep this morning about Cody, okay?"

She glanced at him, then nodded. "Okay. Yeah. You're right."

Even blubbery bully-boy Teddy Bishop and his pal Joey had shown up—Jack figured they were here more for the day off than out of any concern for Cody.

Many in the crowd were drinking coffee or sodas and munching donuts or breakfast sandwiches—the Krauszer's down on the highway must have done a land-office business this morning—and most were talking, smiling, some even laughing.

Come on, people, he felt like saying. This isn't a picnic. We're here to search for a kid who's most likely dead.

He noticed a couple of arms waving in the air from the far side of the crowd and recognized Karina and Cristin. Karina was wearing her engineer's cap again.

His spirits lifted at the sight of her. As Jack waved back, Eddie said, "I think she's got the *haaaaahts* for you, Jack."

"Hots?" Weezy said, straightening and looking around like a dog that just heard a strange noise. "For Jack? Who?"

"Karina Haddon." Eddie pointed. "Right over there."

Weezy looked and said, "Oh. She's on our bus." She frowned at Jack. "She doesn't look your type."

Swell.

"What's my type?"

"I don't know," she said, looking a bit flustered. "I just didn't think it would be a hippie."

"She's not a hippie."

"Well, she dresses the part. Remember what you told me about me being a goth because I liked black—"

"And Bauhaus and Siouxsie."

"'If it walks like a duck and quacks like a duck . . .'"

"I hardly know her."

"But do you *like* her?" The answer seemed important to her.

Could she be having the same reaction to Karina that he had to Carson?

Jealousy? he wondered.

Most likely not. But something close. A queasy, off-course feeling that things might be changing between them, that they might lose the special bond they'd shared for so many years. High school, with all the new people it was pushing into their lives—pushing *between* them—seemed to threaten that bond.

Was she now getting a taste of that too?

Everything seemed in flux—people dying, people and things disappearing . . . he didn't like change. He wanted everything to stay the same—wished Johnson could be kept in a bottle like Kandor in Superman's Fortress of Solitude.

Well, Jack wasn't going to lie to her. "Yeah. I like her. She's cool."

Weezy stared in Karina's direction.

"Cool?"

2

The state cops and the deputies divided the crowd into groups. Jack had to decide whether to go with Tim Davis's group, or edge over and hang with Karina. His mother and her friends were directed toward another group. He settled on Tim. Weezy and Eddie were there and he felt they should stick together. After all, they knew Cody. Karina and Cristin did not.

"All right, listen up, everybody," Tim said to the thirty or so people gathered around his patrol car. He had a map spread out on the hood. "We took the area around where we found Cody's bike and divided it into a grid. Our group has been assigned a specific square of that grid. We're going to walk out to the spot, and when we get there I'll show you what to do."

He took the lead on the fire trail that led away from Johnson. People followed in groups of two and three, speaking in low voices. The party atmosphere had dissipated.

"I hope we find something," Eddie said.

Weezy folded her arms tight across her chest. "I know what I *don't* want to find."

"What?"

"Cody."

"I second that," Jack said. "Been there, done that, don't want to do it again."

He couldn't help thinking about finding the body in the mound last month. What a shock—hadn't expected to dig up anything like that. He and Weezy and the rest of Johnson were still dealing with the fallout from that discovery in different ways and to different degrees. No doubt about who it had affected most: Weezy.

But today was different. Today they'd be *looking* for a body. Sure, everyone hoped and prayed Cody was okay, but did anyone here actually believe they'd find him alive? Jack didn't. He hoped for the best, but he knew the chances were approaching zero.

Yet, if Cody's body was here, he hoped someone would find it today and stop the Bockmans' nightmare. If they missed it, the torture of not knowing would go on and on.

But not knowing allowed for hope. He wondered which was worse—eternal fruitless hope, or the short, sharp shock of the truth?

Jack didn't know. He did know that if Cody Bockman's body was found today, he wanted someone else to find it.

They turned south off the fire trail and wound their way along deer trails through trees and underbrush. Jack had worn jeans and a long-sleeve rugby shirt. Weezy and Eddie, both seasoned veterans of Pinelands exploration, also wore long sleeves. Jack felt sorry for the neos who had come with short-sleeved and even sleeveless tops—looking to boost their summer tan before fall? They were in for a morning of scratches from the brush and bites from mosquitoes and greenhead flies.

When they reached the designated area, Tim had his people line up side by side, facing south. Next he had everyone stretch their arms straight out from their sides, then move away until each person was touching fingertips with the person on either side. Weezy stood to Jack's left, Eddie to his right.

"Okay," Tim said through a bullhorn. *"Everyone pick out a landmark straight ahead of them. Remember that landmark.*

Now start walking toward it, but concentrate on the ground. Eyeball every inch, looking for anything that didn't originate in the Pines. If you see anything—anything, *even if it looks like litter—give a holler. Same with any tree you're passing: Examine the bark and look up into the branches. Again, if you see something, give a holler. Now, whenever you hear someone holler, stop where you are so I can go check it out and tag it if it seems like it's worth looking into. Got that?"*

He repeated the instructions, then finished with: *"Be alert. His bike was found just east of here. We may get lucky."*

All depends on what you mean by "lucky," Jack thought.

Tim started the line moving. The going was slow—lots of trees in the way. Each had to be checked up and down, all the way around. That made it hard to keep moving in a straight line. Open areas were few and far between, and last night's rain would have washed away whatever tracks had been left behind.

Someone far to the right yelled. Everyone stopped and waited as Tim hustled over, checked it out, then used a slim bamboo stick with a little Day-Glo red pennant on top to mark the spot.

"All right," he bullhorned. *"Let's get moving again. Take your time. No rush. The last thing we want to do is miss something."*

As Jack began walking and searching, word filtered down from the right that someone had found an old, flattened Wawa coffee cup. Probably litter. Good thing Old Man Foster posted his land. If people camped around here, there'd be no end to the junk the searchers would be finding.

He wondered if anyone had asked Foster's permission. Probably not. No one seemed to know where to find him. And anyway, how could he have said no? Even if he had, the search would have gone on anyway.

Another yell, this time from the left. Another stop and wait as Tim planted another flag. After they were moving again, people passed word of the discovery down the line.

"Someone found a child's sneaker," Weezy told him when the news reached her.

"Just one?"

Weezy shrugged. "'*A*' sneaker is what I heard."

"Boy's or girl's?"

She rolled her eyes. "They didn't say."

They kept moving, searching. By the time the group had finished combing its square of the grid, Jack had found nothing. At the end they came upon another group finishing a neighboring square. No sign of Cody there either.

While people broke into chattering groups, Jack made his way back toward where the sneaker had been found. He spotted Tim squatting by a flag, speaking into a walkie-talkie as he studied a small sneaker half buried in sand. His back was turned but Jack could hear him loud and clear.

"Look, it's a red-on-white Keds and it's a kid's size five—just like the mother told us. Get a lab team out here. This could be it."

Jack's stomach coiled. Aw, no.

A faint garble crackled from the receiver, then Tim said, "Okay. Roger and out."

He rose and turned, then froze when he saw Jack.

"What are you doing here?"

"Wanted to see the sneaker. Is it . . . is it Cody's?"

"Can't say."

"But you said it fits the description."

Tim's face gave nothing away. "You weren't supposed to hear that. And even if it does, Keds sells a zillion sneakers like that."

"Yeah, but it's the right size and color and not far from where Cody's bike was found. What are the odds it's *not*?"

Tim sighed. "Don't go blabbing about this, okay?"

"You know I don't blab."

"See that you don't."

Jack squatted for a closer look at the soaked sneaker where it lay on its side, half-filled with wet sand.

"How—?"

"Don't touch it!"

Jack bit back a *duh!*—he'd seen enough cop shows to know you didn't touch evidence—and instead said, "Wasn't going to. How come there's only one?"

"Do I look like the Amazing Carnac?"

Tim was sounding testy.

"But where's the rest of him?"

"If I knew that, do you think I'd be here jawboning with you?"

Something in Tim's tone made Jack glance up at him. He realized he looked exhausted.

"I was only asking."

Tim puffed out his cheeks. "Sorry, Jack. Not much sleep since he disappeared. Johnson's on my circuit and I feel kind of responsible."

"You'll find him." Jack wished he could believe it.

"I've got a feeling that if we do, it will be by accident. All this damn rain washes away trace evidence. And check out that sneak—looks like it's been there for days. Chances of the lab boys getting something off it are slim to none."

"What about the circus?"

Tim shook his head. "They've been as cooperative as can be. We've been all over the grounds, the tents, the trailers—nothing."

"Did you know that a kid disappeared at one of their stops in Michigan?"

Tim stared at him. "What? Where did you hear that?"

Jack told him what the canvas boss had said.

"Well, he didn't tell us anything about it. Damn. Tomorrow's their last night. Then they pack up and head to their next stop. I'd better check into this." He pulled out a notebook. "Did this guy happen to say where in Michigan?"

Jack shook his head. "No. Just Michigan."

As he watched Tim write, he said, "What about the Klenke house?"

Tim shook his head. "First place we looked. Been back twice. Nothing. But I gotta tell you, the second day I was in there, boy, did it stink. The first and third day, fine. But the second—awful. Could almost make you believe the stories about it being haunted." When he finished jotting he looked up. "How's med school treating your sister?"

"She loves it."

"Smartest girl I ever knew." He grinned. "I guess I should be calling her a 'woman' these days. Tell her I was asking for her."

"Sure."

Jack realized Deputy Tim still had a thing for Kate. They'd dated for almost a year, then stopped. No big breakup. They were still friends and talked now and then. He wondered what happened to them.

Tim started walking back toward the group. "Gotta go play mother hen. I know you three can find your way back, but I don't know about the rest. Don't want someone else turning up lost. Remember: Mum's the word."

Jack was turning to follow him when he saw a figure lurking in the trees, staring at him.

3

Jack froze, remembering the incident in the Vivinos' yard last night, but no stink stung his nose and this looked like a kid.

Then he recognized him . . . that tall, skinny piney kid who'd got in Jake Shuett's face. Had a weird name.

Coffin . . . Levi Coffin.

"Levi!" Jack called as the kid turned away.

The kid kept going so Jack started after him.

"Levi, wait up!"

Levi stopped and turned to face him. His expression was flat, his mismatched eyes cold.

"What you want?"

"Just wanted to talk. I'm—"

"I know who you are." His accent sounded almost Southern. "What you wanna talk to an 'inbred' for?"

"Hey, no fair." Jack stopped before him. "That wasn't me. Never was, never will be."

"You sit with him. You get your laughs on us?"

"Come on. Lighten up. Can't always choose who sits at your table. You know that."

"Yeah, truth in that. What you want?"

"Just wondering if you were in the search. I didn't see you."

"Been doin' our own search."

That was heartening. No one knew these woods better than a piney.

"And?"

"He ain't around."

That shook Jack. "He's not in the Pines at *all*?"

"Not in this end. Least not as far as we can tell. Someone or something might've got him and carried him off, but he ain't here now."

"Some*thing*? You mean, like a big stinky bear or—"

"Stink." Levi's eyes widened and he leaned closer. "What you know about stink?"

Jack told him about the hulking silhouette Weezy, Eddie, and he had seen in the Pines last month.

"You know what it is?"

Levi shook his head. "No one does, but when we smell it, we run. You smell it again, you do the same—like the hounds of hell're after you."

Jack thought about the odor in the Vivinos' yard. Had something come after Sally?

Taking a shot in the dark, Jack pointed toward the east and said, "Is it connected to that pyramid out there?"

Levi followed his point, then smiled. "Figured it'd be only a matter of time before you and your girlfriend tumbled onto that."

"She's not my girlfriend, and how do you know—?"

"We spot you two now and again. Saw you and her messin' with Jed Jameson's traps. You might wanna be careful about that. He's real mean."

Jack already knew that.

"But what about the pyramid? What is it—or what was it?"

Levi shrugged. "No one knows. But Saree says stay away, so we do. You might wanna do the same."

"Who's Saree?"

"One of us."

By the way Levi said "us," Jack had a feeling he wasn't talking about pineys in general, or family. More like something much closer even than family.

"I don't understand."

Levi smiled and turned away. "And you never will. Stay in your town and leave the Pines to us. You've got your place and we've got ours. Best to keep it that way. Especially tonight."

"But—"

He waved a hand without looking back. Jack got the message: conversation over.

He watched him disappear into the trees.

Especially tonight . . . The equinox. He and Weezy had plans for a little trip into the Pines tonight. Maybe the smart thing to do would be to call it off.

Fat chance.

4

"Hey, Walt!"

On his way down Quakerton Road toward USED, Jack spotted Walt rolling a mower over the lawn of the VFW post on the other side of the street. He veered his bike in that direction.

He skidded to a stop before the post—really a converted ranch house. The sign over the door read: VETERANS OF FOREIGN WARS—JOHNSON MEMORIAL POST. He stood his bike on the sidewalk and walked over.

Walt looked up from the mower. His eyes held their usual glassy look from his applejack. The neck of a pint bottle poked up from one of the pockets of his fatigue jacket.

"Hey, Jack. Saw you at the search." He scratched his beard with leather-gloved fingers and shook his shaggy head. "Shame we didn't find that poor kid. People found a lot of stuff, but most of it was junk. Maybe something will give them a clue, but it doesn't look good."

"Our group found a kid's sneaker, but who knows . . ." Jack let the subject drift off as he checked out the post's ragged grass, badly in need of cutting. "That still looks pretty wet."

"Yeah, I know, but I gotta get it done today because they're talking about more rain tomorrow, and tomorrow night's the smoker."

Right. The fourth Thursday of every month was smoker night. *Boys' night out,* Dad liked to call it, with emphasis on the first word. He never went. He'd tried it and didn't like it. Not his cup of tea, as he liked to say.

Jack knew what went on: cigars and cards and drinking and porno films. He didn't think it would be his cup of tea—especially the cigar part—but he'd sure like to try it once. He'd heard about porno films, talked to some kids who'd seen some, but had never seen one himself. He was curious.

The smoker . . . a whole bunch of the area's vets, from up Tabernacle way down to Shamong, would be here tomorrow night.

And then Mr. Bainbridge's voice from the other night echoed through his head.

. . . we finally got rid of those old eight-millimeters. We've got a VCR now . . .

Yes! Show a tape of Freeholder-wannabe Al Vivino in action to a whole roomful of his VFW buddies. He'd *never* live that down.

But first Jack needed a tape.

Last night's close call at the Vivinos' had left him sort of uncertain about going back for another try. It seemed risky and kind of stupid without a plan of what to do with the video if and when he got it.

But this changed everything.

"Hey, you know, Walt," he said, nodding toward the post, "I've never been inside. What's it look like?"

"Not much to see. Ground floor here's got the meeting room and the office. Downstairs is the rec room with the bar. Want me to show you around sometime?"

"Hey, that'd be great. I—"

"Good day, gentlemen."

Jack looked around and saw Mrs. Clevenger and her dog standing a few feet behind them.

How had she got there? When he'd walked up to Walt she'd been nowhere in sight. Now she and her mutt were practically on top of him.

"Oh, um, hi, Mrs. Clevenger."

As usual she wore her long black dress and scarf.

"Did Walter speak to you about staying out of the Pines?"

"I told him," Walt said. "Weezy too."

It seemed lots of people wanted them away from the Pines tonight. Didn't they know it was like waving a red flag before a bull?

Jack said, "Because of the equinox? What's so special about the equinox?"

She pursed her lips. "It's a time when a delicate balance is temporarily upset . . . things flux, and then a new balance is achieved. You do not want to be in the wrong place at the wrong time during the autumnal equinox."

Did she call that an answer?

"Excuse me, Mrs. Clevenger, but I have no idea what you just said."

She smiled. "I'm afraid that's as specific as I can get. Suffice it to say in this hemisphere the autumnal equinox is when the dark supersedes the light, and dominates it to varying degrees for the next six months. Odd phenomena occur during the changeover."

"Like what?"

She smiled again. "I'm afraid 'odd' will have to do. But consider it a gross understatement."

Why couldn't she give him a straight answer? Then again, he couldn't remember her ever giving him a straight answer.

"Thanks," he said. "I guess."

She and her dog stared at him. "Heed me and stay close to home. Do I make myself clear?"

"Yeah. Sure. Very."

He was about to ask her more but she turned to Walt and gripped his arm.

"I must speak to you, Walter." She looked at Jack. "It's a private matter, if you don't mind, Jack."

He backed away a step. "Oh, sure. That's okay. I've got to get over to the store anyway. Later for the tour, Walt?"

"Sure, Jack, catch you later."

I seem to be into tours lately, he thought as he moved back toward his bike—slowly . . . as slowly as he could, straining to hear what Mrs. Clevenger had to say. She'd lowered her voice but he was still able to capture most of her words.

"I need you to stop this for a while."

A quick glance back showed her tapping the cap of the bottle in his pocket.

"What for?" he said at higher volume. "You know what can happen if I do."

"That's exactly why I'm asking you to stop."

"It's gonna wake up." A hint of a whine crept into his voice. "I don't want to wake it up."

Wake up what? What was he talking about?

"You may be needed in the next day or so."

"Aw, no. You know it hurts me."

"I do know. And I would not ask you if I did not think it very important."

"But—"

"Would I ever try to hurt you?"

"No."

"Then do this for me."

A sigh. "Okay, okay. Who?"

"Someone you'll want to help."

Jack reached his bike. To stall further, he squatted and pretended to fiddle with the pedals.

"Can you at least tell me when?"

"I don't know yet. Tomorrow, I think. I'll know more as the time nears. Right now it's all a tangle of intersecting possibilities. You might not be needed at all."

"Wouldn't that be great."

"Yes. That would be best for all concerned."

Unable to delay any longer, Jack kicked back the stand and hopped on his bike. As he rode away, Mrs. Clevenger's words stayed in his head, tickling his brain. Why was she telling Walt to stop drinking? Because he might need to help someone in the next day or so? What did that mean? What kind of help? Really, Walt was a lovable guy, but he wasn't good for much but drinking.

Or was it simply a loony conversation between the town's two looniest characters?

5

Jack's resolve to see this through, so strong this afternoon outside the VFW post, had begun to slip with the fading of the daylight. Only Tony's dream words pushed him out the door and up 206 to the Vivino house.

Just as he had last night, Jack left his bike on the far side of Mr. Rosen's trailer, stole across his backyard, and squeezed through the hedge onto the Vivino property. He was about to settle behind the same bush when he heard Mr. Vivino's voice from inside. He was shouting.

Jack froze and squeezed his eyes shut. He didn't want to see this. He wanted to be back home in his room reading Stephen King or H. P. Lovecraft or *The Spider*, lost in a book where the horrors and dangers could be stopped in their tracks simply by closing the covers. Not here where real people were feeling real pain and real fear and he was powerless to help.

He felt the weight of the camcorder in his hand and realized he wasn't powerless.

Clenching his teeth and ignoring the crawling in his gut, Jack turned on the camcorder as he edged forward and peeked in the window where the voices seemed the loudest. He gasped when he saw Mr. Vivino behind his wife, holding her in an armlock again and pressing her against a wall.

"I'm sick of it, goddammit! Sick of it!"

Jack's hands shook as he raised the camcorder, sighted through the viewfinder, and hit the record button. A little red REC lit in the upper left-hand corner of the image just as

Mr. Vivino pulled her back and then slammed her against the wall. She had her eyes squeezed shut as pain distorted her features.

"How many times do I have to tell you not to—"

"Stop-it-stop-it-stop-it!" Sally screamed as she rushed into the room and clung to her father's arm. "Stop-it, Daddy!"

A flick of his arm shoved her away. She tripped over her feet as she stumbled back and hit the floor.

Mrs. V screamed, "Sally!" and twisted like a tigress in her husband's grasp, elbowing him in the gut.

He *oomph*ed, but instead of letting go, he threw her to the floor and kicked her, screaming, "Don't you *ever* hit me!"

Jack was so shaken by the violence he lost his grip on the camcorder, allowing it to slip from his grasp and *clunk* against the windowsill.

Mr. Vivino whirled toward the window. "Wha—? Goddammit, someone's at the window!"

Didn't have to think, didn't have to decide—Jack spun and raced toward the hedge and dove headfirst through the branches into Mr. Rosen's yard. They scratched his face and caught on his clothes but he landed on the far side before Mr. Vivino saw him.

He hoped.

Over his shoulder and through the branches he saw Mr. Vivino lunge into view at the window.

"He went next door! I'll get the son of a—!"

He disappeared and Jack jumped to his feet. The crazy madman was coming for him!

He looked around. What to do? His first instinct was to run around to the other side of the trailer, grab his bike, and race like mad out of here. But if he tried that he risked Mr. Vivino spotting him.

Had to hide. But where?

Like last night, too early for the moon, so he had darkness on his side. He saw the big propane tank nestled against the side of the trailer. He looked under and around it but saw no space big enough to hide.

A door slammed at the Vivino house.

"I get my hands on you, I'm gonna tear you apart!"

Oh, crap!

No place to hide on the ground, how about up? No trees—but the trailer had a flat roof.

Swinging the camcorder around so its strap encircled his throat and the cam hung between his shoulder blades, Jack hopped up on the propane tank and levered himself onto the roof where he immediately flattened himself against the damp sheet metal—just as Mr. Vivino fought his way through the hedge.

Swearing and cursing in a steady stream, he moved to the front of the trailer and started banging on the door.

"Rosen! Rosen, you nosy old bastard! Was that you? Were you peeking in my window?"

He kept pounding and shouting, but no one but Jack was listening. The only house within earshot was Mr. Vivino's own.

Finally he stopped, and Jack had an awful thought.

My bike!

If he searched around the other side of the house he'd find it. He wouldn't recognize the BMX as Jack's, but eventually he'd find out.

But no. Muttering to himself, he headed back to his own yard. Jack didn't wait around as he had last night. He eased himself down to the propane tank and from there to the ground. He ran around to the other side of the trailer, grabbed his bike, and began pedaling north on 206—away from Johnson. He'd go about a mile, then double back. He'd look like he was returning from the circus.

The circus . . . He wondered if the sheriff's department was looking into the Michigan thing and if they'd found anything. He was glad he'd mentioned it to Tim. He'd helped there.

He touched the camcorder dangling from his neck. And he could help even more here. All he had to do was find a way to let the vets see this tape at their smoker tomorrow night.

A tall order, one he had only a vague idea of how to fill.

But he'd find a way. He owed it to Tony. But more important, he owed it to Sally and her mom. They were the ones living through that hell.

6

Later on, back home, he hid the camcorder in his room, then went back and stuck his head into the living room where his folks were watching *Remington Steele*. Just another private eye show to Jack, and not a very good one, but he suspected his mother liked watching Pierce Brosnan. And Dad probably didn't mind looking at Stephanie Zimbalist either.

He said good night and headed for his room. He closed the door and sat on the bed. He'd promised to meet Weezy for their equinox excursion into the Pines but didn't much feel like it. After what he'd seen tonight, he wanted nothing more than to pull the covers over his head and hide. If he slept, he wouldn't have to think about it. But he'd probably dream about it.

Maybe the simple, natural purity of the Barrens would clear his head.

He climbed out the window. As he eased his bike from the garage and walked it toward the street, he wondered at the strange way events had been connecting lately.

If Weezy had never found the pyramid in the mound, Jack wouldn't have started digging to find another, and wouldn't have found the corpse. If he hadn't found the corpse, Freeholder Haskins might still be alive. If Mr. Haskins were alive, Mr. Vivino wouldn't be running for his vacant seat and wouldn't have visited Jack's house with Sally Saturday night, awakening memories of Tony. And without those memories, Jack might not have peeked into the Vivino backyard Sunday night. And if he hadn't done that, this tape wouldn't exist.

A strange sequence of events that could be traced directly back to the pyramid. So many incidents—including all those deaths—circled that mysterious little pyramid.

Where would it end? Would getting it back change things for the better? Or make them worse?

Maybe if they got it back he could convince Weezy to rebury it in the mound where they'd found it. Put the genie back in the bottle, so to speak.

Yeah, he thought with a shake of his head. She'll go for that. Uh-huh.

7

They met up at the lightning tree and Weezy led him into the Pines. The bright, rising moon lit the trails while casting deep shadows beneath the trees.

"Look!" she cried after they had traveled no more than a hundred yards or so. "Lumens!"

Three pine lights, varying in size from a Ping-Pong ball to a basketball, drifted in a line along the treetops to their right, heading south.

Mr. Collingswood had mentioned them and Jack had seen some last month when those mysterious men had been excavating the mound. No one knew what they were. He'd heard them explained as St. Elmo's fire or swamp gas, even heard they were the souls of dead pineys back for a visit. Mrs. Clevenger's words about "odd phenomena" came back to him, and how "odd" might be a gross understatement.

Curiosity urged him to follow, but he hesitated, hearing Walt and Mrs. Clevenger's warnings about being in the wrong place during the time of the equinox.

Then he saw another pair of softball-size lights skid by overhead, moving in the same direction as the others, and that clinched it.

"Let's go!"

Following wasn't easy. The firebreak trails didn't always match the direction of the lights, but whenever they came to a fork, they angled toward the lights. Luckily the lumens didn't seem to be in a terrible hurry to get wherever they were going, if anywhere. But Jack sensed a direction, almost as if they had a purpose. But of course they had no purpose. They were just balls of light.

As he and Weezy traveled, more and more lights joined the procession until they were following a couple of dozen or more. Some moved more quickly than others, zigzagging past the slower ones, like cars on a highway. They seemed to have a definite purpose now, gliding through the dark, weaving from tree to tree along the topmost branches as if following signposts.

"Jack! Isn't this wonderful?"

He wasn't so sure. He felt a gnawing sensation in his chest. Had anyone ever seen anything like this? Then he noticed the silence. The Barrens were a noisy place, with animals, birds, and insects constantly hooting and crying and chirping, the breeze rustling the bushes. All that was gone now. Even the crickets were quiet. It seemed like the whole place was holding its breath.

The good thing was he didn't feel threatened. The bad thing was he didn't know what to expect.

The thing he least expected was for their line of lights to meet up and merge with another line from the east. But it did, just up ahead of them.

They mingled awhile, then began to flow toward the south.

All except one . . .

A soccer-ball-size light stayed behind, then began drifting their way. Jack noticed Weezy's rapt expression as it neared. He felt a strange tightening in his chest. He gripped her upper arm.

"I don't like this."

"I do."

It sank to about a dozen feet off the ground and hovered before them.

"The lumen . . . it's humming, Jack! Like music."

Jack heard a high-pitched hum. His hackles rose and his skin tingled as if the air was charged with electricity. He broke out in a cold sweat.

"Let's get out of here."

But Weezy didn't budge, even as the lumen came closer. She reached out a hand, as if to touch it, but Jack snatched it back.

"Don't!"

"Why not? I—*ew*! It smells."

Jack caught it too, a sour stench somewhere between stale sweat and spoiled meat. It turned his stomach and caused a growing sense of dread. He'd smelled it before and he knew what it meant.

They weren't alone.

"It's not the lumen."

Where was it? He gave a frantic twist left and then right, but didn't see anything. The stink said it was close by. Levi had said to run if he smelled it—*like the hounds of hell're after you*. But which way? *Think!*

Wait. If he was smelling it, that meant it was upwind. He calmed himself, stood statue still, sensing the breeze.

There—faint against the left side of his face, to the east. He turned in that direction and froze as he spotted a dark, hulking shape standing half in, half out of the shadows of the treeline. It seemed to be watching them and the lumen. Was this the thing that had chased Mr. Collingswood up a tree?

Jack pressed a finger over Weezy's lips and pointed. In the glow from the lumen he saw her eyes widen and felt her stiffen as she saw the shape.

Without warning, the lumen rose and darted off toward the south, following its kind. Jack didn't wait to see what the shape would do.

He slapped Weezy on the back and whispered, "Go!"

They were only halfway off their bikes. He hopped the rest of the way onto his seat and began pumping the pedals for all he was worth. He heard a hiss and then something heavy crashing through the underbrush behind him as the tires of his BMX slipped and skidded in the sandy soil. He heard Weezy whimpering in fear as her tires did the same. Finally they caught and he almost screamed with relief as he began moving.

He saw Weezy beside him, grunting with effort.

"Don't look back!" he said. "Just go-go-go!"

The slightest wobble in one of their front tires now could send them into a skidding crash.

But Jack looked back. He couldn't help it.

Something big and dark was racing his way through the moon-dappled underbrush. He couldn't tell if it was running in a crouch or on all fours, but it was fast and it was closing.

Jack put every ounce of strength he had into his legs, pushing as hard as he'd ever pushed against those pedals.

"Go, Weez! Give it everything!"

At least they were headed west, toward Johnson. He just prayed they'd make it.

Why hadn't he listened? When was he going to learn?

He kept pedaling, leaning over his handlebars, and urging the bike forward. He heard an angry screech but didn't look back. After traveling somewhere between a quarter and half a mile, and not hearing anything more behind him for a while, he chanced another glance. When he saw an empty trail, relief flooded him.

"I think we're safe," he said, "but keep going."

They didn't slow their pace until they reached Old Town.

"What *was* that?" Weezy said, panting as they coasted past the lightning tree.

Jack's sweat was cooling as he caught his breath.

"A bear . . . had to be a black bear like Tim said."

"But it didn't roar or even growl."

Right. Instead it had hissed and come after them, then screeched—probably when it had given up the chase.

"A bear," Jack said. "A weird bear."

"You're kidding yourself, Jack. That wasn't a bear. I'll bet it's connected to the pyramid back in the Pines."

"Weezy—"

"Tomorrow, Jack. We're going out there tomorrow."

"Okay," he said reluctantly. "But in daylight—in broad daylight."

She laughed. "If you're expecting an argument from me, forget it." She sobered. "You know . . . they say Marcie Kurek ran away, but what if she wandered into the Pines and was grabbed by that thing?"

Jack shook his head. "Then I don't think we'll ever see or hear from her again."

He followed her to her house—he wasn't simply going to assume she'd get home safe as he had with Cody—and they split with a silent wave at her driveway. A few minutes later Jack coasted into his yard. He slipped in through his bedroom window, then pulled out the videotape. In the hallway he crept to the bottom of the stairs and listened. He heard the sound of the TV drifting down from his folks' room. They tended to watch the eleven o'clock news, followed by Johnny Carson's monologue on *The Tonight Show*, then shut down and call it a day.

He stole to the downstairs TV, turned it on, then the videotape player, but lowered the sound to zero. He inserted the tape, rewound, and hit PLAY. As soon as the scene of Mr. Vivino with his wife in an armlock lit the screen, Jack stopped. He couldn't bear to watch it again, but had to be sure he'd caught the incident before proceeding to the next step.

He rewound the cassette to its beginning and ejected it. After turning off the TV and the player, he hid the tape in his room.

What a day. He wanted to talk to someone about it, but couldn't mention taping the Vivinos to *anyone*. And as for what he'd witnessed with Weezy, his dad would go ballistic if he knew he'd been in the Pines at night. He didn't like him in there during the day.

He went to the window and stared out at the starlit sky. Looked like a long night ahead.

THURSDAY

1

The videotape cassette had been burning a hole through Jack's backpack all day at school. Or at least it felt that way. Now at last, after a seeming eternity, he was returning to Johnson.

He'd found it almost infinitely difficult to wave to Sally and Mrs. V this morning as they waited across the street at the elementary bus stop. She'd stood there in her dark glasses and long-sleeved blouse, seeming to pierce him with her gaze as if she knew.

Did she? No way. He'd been out in the dark, she'd been inside in the light. She couldn't have seen him.

So why had she been staring at him?

Maybe she hadn't. Maybe just staring through him and thinking of a better life, a life without her husband.

Once in school Jack had hidden the cassette at the rear of his locker's top shelf. He'd checked on it a number of times during the course of the day. He didn't know why he was so paranoid. No one but he knew it existed.

He stepped off the bus and headed directly to the VFW post. This was it: Do or die. He had to find a way to get this onto the screen tonight. If he failed he'd have to wait until the next smoker. He couldn't bear the thought of Sally and her mother suffering through another month of what he'd seen last night.

When he reached the post he found the front door wide open. The smell of strong detergent wafted from within.

"Hello? Anyone here?"

No answer.

Almost too good to be true to find the place open and empty. He could just waltz down to the rec room and do his thing—whatever that might turn out to be.

He stepped inside and called again.

"Hello?"

To his dismay, a familiar voice, accompanied by the sound of feet on stairs, answered.

"I'm coming, I'm coming." Walt appeared from a stairwell and smiled when he saw Jack. "Hey, man. What's up?"

"I'm cashing in my rain check for the tour."

"Oh, hey, I was just about to start mopping the floor downstairs and—"

"Just a quick look?"

As Walt hesitated, Jack noticed that his eyes were clearer than he'd ever seen them.

Then he remembered: Mrs. Clevenger asked him to stop drinking. With all that had gone on since yesterday afternoon, Jack had forgotten about the conversation he'd overheard.

She'd wanted him to stop because he might be "needed." What did she expect Walt to do?

Whatever, it looked like he'd listened to her. Jack noticed that his gloved hands were shaking. Nervous? Or did he need a drink?

Walt shrugged then. "Sure. Why not?"

Jack suffered through the ground-floor tour—what did he care about the meeting room and the office? Finally Walt led him down to where he wanted to be: the basement.

At the moment the rec room was a big open space with a bare floor of dirty vinyl tile. A mahogany bar with beer spigots up front and mirrored shelves behind ran three-quarters the length of one wall. A TV sat on a low cabinet under a squat window. All the chairs and tables were stacked in a corner. A battered wringer bucket sat in the middle of the floor with a mop handle jutting toward the ceiling.

Walt gestured to the space. "I don't know why they want the floor mopped before the smokers—these guys are real slobs when it comes to keeping beer in their cups. But if that's what they want, that's what they get."

Jack wandered over to the TV cabinet and opened the doors. He wanted to make sure he'd heard Mr. Bainbridge right about the new VCR.

"What's up, Jack?" he heard Walt say behind him.

"Just checking out your electronics."

Yep. There it sat: a brand-new Panasonic. And next to it a couple of videotape boxes labeled *Electric Lady* and *Pizza Girls* with scantily clad women on the covers. He tore his gaze away from them as something clicked in his brain. He looked back at the tape player and his heart nearly stopped when he saw the three letters following the brand logo.

VHS.

"No!"

He checked again. No mistake. It said VHS and the tape slot was definitely too big.

"Something wrong, Jack? You okay?"

He was anything but okay, and something was definitely and terribly wrong as he realized what he'd done.

I screwed up! All that risk for nothing!

He'd recorded the Vivinos on a Betamax cassette. It wouldn't play on a VHS.

"I'm okay," he managed to say. "Just remembered something I'd forgotten." He turned and started for the door. "I'll finish the tour later."

"Ain't nothin' left to see."

Jack didn't reply as he hurried upstairs and out into the fresh air.

"Jerk!" he whispered as he broke into a trot up Quakerton Road. "You complete *jerk*!"

Mr. Rosen had bought a Betamax camcorder—that was why it had been cheap. Jack had been so tickled to have a video camera at his disposal, he hadn't paid attention to what kind. And why should he, considering the VCR in his own house was a Beta?

Dad's doing. Years ago he'd bought a Betamax, supposedly better than the competing VHS model. Maybe it was, but it lost out to the other format because VHS tapes recorded longer. So most folks used VHS these days.

But not Dad. He insisted Betamax was better and refused to switch until the current machine died. Why change if it recorded and played back and did everything a VCR should?

So of course the Vivino tape had played perfectly on his home machine last night—a Beta cassette in a Beta player.

But it would *not* play on the VFW machine.

He had to find some way to turn this around.

2

"Hey, I don't know, Jack," Eddie said.

"Just for thirty minutes," Jack said as he went about disconnecting the Connell family's VCR from their TV. "Not a second longer, I swear."

"But I still don't get why you need it."

"Just running a little experiment between Beta and VHS."

In a way that was true. Sort of. Not so much an experiment as a desperate, last-ditch effort to salvage Operation Vivino.

"What kind of experiment?"

"I'll let you know if it works." He finished unscrewing the VCR's coaxial cable. "Until then, have you got a blank tape I can borrow? I'll replace it later."

Eddie fished in a drawer and came up with one still in the wrapper.

Perfect.

"Need any help?"

"That's okay. You hang here and I'll be right back."

Tucking the VCR under his arm, Jack hurried out the front door toward home. He wanted to run but didn't dare risk dropping the Connells' VCR—a VHS model.

The only good thing so far about today was that it was another of his mother's volunteer days at the hospital. He had the house to himself until she came home. He wasn't exactly sure when that would be so he had to hurry.

Once inside he dropped to his knees before the Betamax—already partially unhooked—and went to work.

First, he plugged in the VHS and attached the cable from its input to the Beta's output. Then he unwrapped the new VHS tape, inserted it, and hit the record button. The Vivino tape was already in the Betamax, so all he had to do was hit PLAY.

He waited ten minutes—the scene he'd caught hadn't lasted even five—then rewound and ejected the tape. After stuffing it in his backpack, he ran outside, hopped on his bike, and began pedaling like mad.

3

"Please be there," Jack muttered as he rolled up the front walk.

His heart sank as he saw the door closed, but he leaped off his bike, letting it fall, and ran up to the front door. He tried the knob and found it open.

"Walt?" he called, stepping inside. "You still here?"

"Still here," came a voice from the stairwell. "Come on down."

Jack did just that and found Walt starting to drag a table across the floor. Jack leaped to his side.

"Let me help you with that."

"Now that the floor's finally dry," Walt said as they carried it to the center of the room, "time to move everything back. This one goes right here. Thanks, Jack."

"No problem. You need help with the rest?"

"That's okay."

"Hey, I'm here. Why not?"

Walt grinned. "Okay. Appreciate that."

As Jack helped drag chairs and tables to wherever Walt said they belonged, his gaze kept drifting to the VCR cabinet. He had to find a way to get in there again.

They were maybe three-quarters finished when a woman's voice echoed down the stairwell.

"Walter? May I speak with you a moment?"

"Huh? Oh, yeah, Mrs. Clevenger." Walt looked at Jack and shrugged. He looked worried. "Be right there."

"Go ahead," Jack said, fighting a grin of triumph. "Take your time. I'll finish up."

As much as Jack would have loved to know what those two were talking about, he had other priorities. So as soon as Walt was out of sight, he grabbed the tape from his backpack and flew to the VCR cabinet. He opened the doors and dumped the *Electric Lady* tape out of its box, then replaced it with his own. His had no label, but he could only hope no one noticed or cared. He snapped it shut and replaced it in the cabinet.

Now . . . what to do with the real tape? He'd have loved to take it home and watch it, but he couldn't play it on his machine. So he slipped it behind the cabinet. Walt was done with moving furniture for the day, so it would be safe for the present.

But the tape he'd replaced it with . . . he hadn't had time to check it, so he didn't even know if the video transfer had been successful. For all he knew, they'd be showing a blank tape tonight.

By the time Walt returned, Jack had all the chairs arranged around the tables.

Walt beamed. "You're a real good guy, Jack, y'know that?"

"Nothing to it. Um, what did Mrs. C want?"

His smile vanished and he looked uneasy. "Not much. She just wants me to hang around somewhere."

"Where?"

"Just . . . around."

Jack could see he was uncomfortable and decided not to push. Besides, he had to get home and straighten out the VCR mess he'd left behind before his mom got home.

"Hey, what time's the smoker start?"

"Oh, guys start wandering in around seven-thirty, but things usually don't get rolling till about eight. Why? No way you can get in."

"Just curious."

Jack glanced at the little window above the TV. He knew where he'd be come eight o'clock. But before that, he and Weezy had a date with a pyramid.

4

They rode toward the Pines, each with a short-handle spade-shovel from his garage held across their handlebars. The sun was sinking but they had better than an hour and a half of light left. Plenty of time.

Passing the lightning tree, he saw Gus Sooy's pickup. He and Walt were leaning against the rear side panel. Walt wasn't drinking and wasn't getting a bottle filled, just seemed to be talking. They both waved and Jack and Weezy waved back.

Was this where Mrs. Clevenger had told Walt to hang out? Was this where he'd be "needed"? For what?

He shook his head. He'd probably never know.

As they neared the spong they picked up speed—they wanted to be a swiftly moving target if that piney started throwing rocks again. But as they passed, Jack saw no sticks jutting toward the sky.

"That piney must have reset his traps," Weezy said.

"And it looks like Mrs. Clevenger hasn't got to them yet. Think we should . . . ?"

Weezy shook her head. "Maybe on the way back. We'll need all the light we can get at the pyramid."

Jack wondered again what would happen if the piney caught Mrs. C springing his traps. She was just an old lady, but that dog of hers, even with three legs, looked like he could inflict a world of hurt on anyone messing with his owner.

They reached the burned-out area and made their way past the ruined mound to the pyramid.

The clearing was eerily silent as Jack checked out the ground for fresh tracks. He found none of any sort, and even the old ones they'd seen before were gone, erased by multiple rains.

They hopped over the low stone wall and squeezed through one of the gaps between the megaliths.

The floor of the cage—if that was what the pyramid was—was no longer underwater, but the sand was still wet. Any trace that he and Weezy had stood here on Saturday was gone. Weezy walked to the four-foot stone post in the center and again traced her fingers along the six-sided indentation in its top.

"If we had the little pyramid we could fit it in here and see what happens."

"Like what?"

"Maybe the sunlight during the equinox hits it at a certain angle and . . ."

"What? We go back in time?"

She smiled. "Never know."

"Until then . . ." Jack looked around. "Where do we start?"

She shrugged. "Anywhere, I guess."

He chose a random spot near the center post and began to dig straight down. Weezy did the same a half dozen feet away.

"I've got a suspicion about this place," she said. "If it's modeled on the little pyramid we found, it should have a base. With all the sand in the Barrens' soil, water percolates through pretty quickly. The standing water in here back on Saturday tells me something was slowing its absorption."

Sure enough—four feet down Jack hit granite. The seventh side. And no doubt carved into its surface somewhere was the seventh symbol—just like on the baby pyramid.

Panting a little and sweating a lot, he took a break. He hadn't paid much attention to what he'd been digging out of the hole, so he turned to that now. Using the side edge of the spade he ran it back and forth over the excavated sand, slowly smoothing it out. And as he did, little bones began to appear.

"Hey, Weez! Look!"

She hurried over and picked up a few for a closer look.

"Not bones. Just pieces—splinters, really."

"How—?"

Then he noticed a larger fragment in the wall of the hole he'd dug. He scraped away the sand packed around it and found it bigger than he'd thought. He yanked on it . . .

And came away with part of a leg bone.

"Ew!" Weezy said, recoiling.

"It's okay. Not human. Deer."

It ran about eighteen inches long and was very slim. During the course of his countless trips into the Pines, Jack had come across a number of dead deer rotted down to their skeletons. From its angled, ball-tipped end he knew what this was.

"A thigh bone. But look. The lower end's broken off."

Weezy leaned closer. "Hey, that looks *gnawed* off. See those scrapes into the bone? They look like teeth marks."

Jack looked around. "How did a deer get in here?"

Weezy gripped his arm. "Jack! Whatever was caged here needed food. It would have been fed by its keepers. The Pines were full of deer. Whatever it was must have eaten every last lick of flesh and then gone after the marrow."

Jack looked at the shattered bones and deep teeth marks. "Strong jaws, sharp teeth."

No question about it now—this structure had been used as a cage. But why so massive?

What had called this place home? Obviously a carnivore, but had it been native to the Pinelands, or had someone imported it? And when? This cage had been here a *long* time.

Weezy's eyes danced with excitement. "Let's keep digging. No telling what we'll find."

But after half an hour or so, shifting their dig sites three times, they'd found nothing but more animal bones. He'd gone about two feet down in his latest dig when the tip of the spade hit something—something bigger than the small bones he'd been finding. He widened the hole and dug around it.

It seemed to be curved, like some sort of arch. He worked his fingers around it, got a grip, and pulled. With a wrench it came free and he found himself holding a jawbone.

He dropped it when he realized it was human.

"Weez! Check it out!"

She hurried over and together they knelt and stared at it. Jack found himself nowhere near as grossed out as he'd have thought he'd be. But then again, this wasn't the first time he'd been through something like this. Yeah, he'd felt a shock, but nothing like when he'd pulled that skull from the mound.

Funny how he'd been thinking just last night about how things seemed to be going in circles, all revolving around the little pyramid, and here he was inside the big pyramid doing the same thing.

With this skull—or part of one—another circle had closed.

"Wh-who could this be?" Weezy said. "It looks so much older than the one in the mound."

Yeah, it did. Not a shred of flesh left on it. And the teeth—browned, cracked, and not a single filling.

For some reason he thought of poor Cody. Chances of finding him alive seemed about zero. Someday someone might be digging in the pines and come up with his little skull.

Jack thrust the thought away and focused on the bone before them.

"Where's the rest of it? And what's it doing in here?"

He dug further and only an inch or so down found upper teeth and the roof of the mouth—the skull was buried upside down. No fillings in the upper teeth either. He cleaned more off, then worked his fingers around it and pulled the skull free.

"Ohmygod!" Weezy cried as he turned it over.

Both stared in shock at the ragged hole in the top of the cranium. Whoever this had been, it looked like his skull had been crushed—cracked open.

She pointed to the edges of the opening. "Are those . . . ?"

Jack looked closer and felt his gut writhe when he saw the gouges around the hole. Just like the tooth marks on the deer bones.

Something had been gnawing at this skull—maybe even ate the brain inside. Sure. Why else chew on a skull?

Now Jack was grossed out. He dropped the skull back into the hole and rose to his feet.

"You think . . . you think that could have been some sort of human sacrifice?"

Weezy was on her feet too, shaking her head. "Maybe one of the keepers got too close at feeding time."

What had gone on here? No question that something with big sharp teeth had been caged in this space, but what?

His neck tingled and he did a quick turn to see if someone was watching. Just his imagination, maybe? He'd been thinking about the captive just now and then he'd got that sensation.

"What's wrong?" Weezy said.

"Nothing."

He didn't want to alarm her. He walked the inside perimeter, peering out at the surrounding trees through one gap after another. No sign of anyone. Or any thing.

But the sensation remained.

Thunder rumbled.

Jack shot a look at the sky and saw that the sun was gone and thunderheads were piling in the west. When had that happened? They must have been so engrossed in their digging they'd failed to notice.

"Are you thinking about that thing that chased us last night?"

He turned to Weezy. "You mean the bear?"

"I mean the *thing*."

"Yeah, I guess I am." He cupped his hands to boost her out of the cage. "Let's get out of here."

She looked relieved. "Took the words right out of my mouth. So much for this pyramid. From now on we concentrate on getting the little one back. But when we do, I'm bringing it back here and setting it in the top of that center column—just to see what happens."

As he boosted her up, he said, "Anyone ever tell you you have a one-track mind?"

"Yeah. I've heard that." She squeezed between two megaliths and turned to offer her hand. "But the truth is I have a *multi*-track mind. It's just that one track's been getting a lot more use than the others lately."

Tell me about it, Jack thought.

5

They beat the storm home by minutes. Jack got in just before his mother and polished off his homework before his father arrived.

The storm was over by the time he finished dinner. He threw on a green Eagles sweatshirt and announced that he was going to take a ride over to the Connells'. Which he did: He rode his bike over to their house, into their driveway, and immediately out again.

Jack hated to lie.

He rode down Quakerton, dodging puddles as he headed for USED. He noticed half a dozen cars parked in front of the VFW, and spotted Walt standing by the front door. He wasn't keen on announcing his presence, but he wanted a closer look at him.

"Walt?" he said, strolling up the walk.

"Huh?" Walt turned and grinned. "Hey, Jack. I hope you don't think you're gettin' in."

In the light from the front of the post Jack could see that Walt's eyes were still clear. Did that mean he might still be "needed"?

"Nah. I don't smoke."

Walt laughed. "Good one."

More cars were pulling up and parking, more vets strolling into the post. If Mr. Bainbridge appeared and spotted Jack, he'd for sure mention it to his father. Best to get out of sight.

He waved and headed back to his bike. "See ya."

He rode across the street to USED where he parked in the shadows alongside the store. He watched the VFW from those shadows until cars stopped pulling up and the front door closed. Then he stole across the street and around to the rear of the post.

The backyard was dark, making it easy to find the basement window: He simply followed the light. Someone had opened it for ventilation and air laden with cigar stink wafted out.

Jack knelt for a look and immediately felt the moisture from the wet grass soak through the knees of his jeans. Crap. He should have thought of that. He bent forward and found himself overlooking the TV set.

A motley group of mixed ages, shapes, and sizes: World War II vets in their late fifties and early sixties, fiftyish Korean survivors like his father and Mr. Bainbridge, and the Vietnam vets in their late thirties and early forties. They all had one thing in common: They'd made it through the fire of war. The experience bonded them. They seemed genuinely to like each other.

Smoke layered the air as some stood around smiling and talking, beers in one hand and stogies in the other, while others sat at the tables shuffling cards or counting out chips.

Boys' night out . . .

He spotted Mr. Vivino in the mix. Jack bet his wife and daughter were glad he was out having a good time and not beating on them. He watched him move through the crowd, grinning, laughing, shaking hands. Mr. Politician. Mr. Freeholder-to-be.

We'll see about that.

Jack backed away a bit when he saw Mr. Bainbridge approach. He bent and disappeared behind the top of the TV.

From this angle Jack couldn't see what he was doing, but guessed he'd opened the cabinet doors. Half a minute later he rose and turned to the crowd.

"All right," he said, holding up the cassette boxes. "Which do we want—*Pizza Girls* or *Electric Lady*?"

Jack tried to project his thoughts through the window: *Electric Lady . . . Electric Lady . . . Electric Lady . . .*

"*Pizza Girls*!" someone cried.

"Yeah!" said another voice. "*Pizza Girls*!"

A chorus of "*Pizza Girls*!" followed.

No-no-no-no!

"*Pizza Girls* it is!"

Jack suppressed a groan as Mr. Bainbridge popped open the box and pulled out the cassette. He realized then he'd made an awful mistake. He had no idea how long these movies ran. What if they showed only one per smoker? He should have hidden *Pizza Girls* behind the cabinet with the *Electric Lady* cassette. Then they would have had to play Jack's tape.

And worse, he still didn't know if his copying had been successful.

He wanted to kick something.

6

Jack paced the dark, narrow aisles of USED. He'd let himself in but left the lights off so he could hang out while the film was running. Every twenty minutes or so he'd sneak over for a peek into the basement. So far, the same every time: some watching the TV and making wisecracks, some playing cards, some in deep conversation. He'd seen Mr. Vivino and Mr. Bishop, the local lawyer and proud father of blubber-butt Teddy, with their heads together. They looked like they were planning a revolution.

The one thing Jack could never see was the TV screen, so he had no idea what the men were watching. At this point, he didn't care. He just wanted it to be over so they could move on to the main attraction.

He stopped at the store counter and grabbed the flashlight Mr. Rosen kept there. He flashed it on one of the clocks. It had been an hour or so since the film started. He doubted it was over yet but guessed he should check again anyway. Who knew? Maybe the tape would jam and they'd start the next film early.

Once more he hurried across the street to the rear of the post. As he peeked in the window he spotted Mr. Bainbridge approaching the TV.

"I think that deserves an Academy Award, don't you?" he said to his buddies.

Some laughed, some clapped, some kept talking, and the cardplayers barely looked up from their hands. Mr. Vivino and Mr. Bishop still plotted in the rear of the room.

Mr. Bainbridge ducked out of sight, then reappeared holding another cassette box.

"Okay!" he announced. "For our next Oscar contender we have *Electric Lady*!"

This was greeted by halfhearted cheers and clapping from the vets, and a silent fist pump from Jack.

Yes!

He settled onto his already wet knees and sent up a prayer that there'd be something on that tape.

Mr. Bainbridge stuck his cigar in his mouth and pulled out the unlabeled cassette. He frowned as he turned it back and forth in his hand.

Put it in the machine, Jack thought. Just. Put. It. In.

Finally he shrugged and did just that.

"Okay! *Electric Lady*—here we go!"

A few scattered claps amid the chatter and then he stepped to the side and watched. Jack couldn't see the screen, only Mr. Bainbridge's face. But soon enough, if Jack's copy had been successful, that face would tell the story.

He studied his expression. The smiling anticipation changed to a puzzled frown. But that didn't mean much—if Jack's tape was blank, that was how he'd react.

Jack watched the frown deepen as the squinty eyes widened and the cigar slipped from loose lips and fell to the floor.

Jack tightened his fists. He could think of only one thing that would cause that sort of reaction.

The video had transferred.

And then he heard the voice from the TV's speakers.

"I'm sick of it, goddammit! Sick of it!"

Mr. Bainbridge gaped. "What the . . . ?"

"How many times do I have to tell you not to—"

"Stop-it-stop-it-stop-it! Stop-it, Daddy!"

He wasn't the only one noticing something wrong. A couple of the men who were seated up front lost their grins as the reaction began to spread through the room like ripples from a stone dropped in a still pond.

"Sally!"

One of the cardplayers noticed and nudged the guys on either side. A player with his back to the screen turned. And then farther into the room people stopped talking and stared at the screen. Gradually the room became a silent sea of stunned faces.

"Don't you ever *hit me!"*

Only Mr. Vivino and Mr. Bishop, against the back wall, continued talking. Eventually they must have realized something was wrong because they clammed up and looked around.

"Wha—? Goddammit, someone's at the window!"

Jack focused on Mr. Vivino's face . . . watched the blood drain from it as his eyes bulged and his jaw dropped.

"What the hell is *that*?" he shouted.

"Well, if I didn't know better," one of the cardplayers said, "I'd say that was you beating the crap out of Cathy."

Mr. Vivino let out a cry like an enraged animal and charged the TV with his arms extended before him, fingers curved into claws.

"Gimme that tape! Gimme that tape!"

But he never reached the set. Hands grabbed him and stopped him. He fought, he twisted, but a grim-faced pair of his fellow vets held him back from the machine.

"Who did this?" he shouted. "Who's the Peeping Tom son of a bitch who did this?"

"Wait a minute! Wait a minute!" said Mr. Bishop, pushing to the front. "I only caught the end there. What's this all about?"

"Rewind it, Kurt," someone said. "I missed it too."

Mr. Bainbridge bent and reached forward. "I could do with another look myself. Not sure I believe what I saw the first time."

"Don't!" Mr. Vivino cried, trying again to struggle free. "It's a lie! It's a fake!"

When Mr. Bainbridge straightened, he had his cigar again. He stepped back to join the rest of the vets who'd crowded forward in a tight, three-deep semicircle before the TV, their eyes fixed on the screen.

Jack didn't need to see. The scene was burned onto his brain. The voices conjured the visuals.

Mrs. V in the painful armlock . . . slammed against the wall . . .

The vets' faces became grimmer.

Sally rushing up . . . getting knocked down.

Gasps from some of the vets.

Aldo Vivino kicking his wife.

The hardened vets wincing.

Finally the angry shout about seeing someone at the window . . . end of video, end of story.

Dead silence in the room as all turned shocked gazes toward Mr. Vivino.

Finally Mr. Bainbridge spoke: "Al . . . Al, my God, you kicked Cathy? *Kicked* her? What the hell's wrong with you?"

Mr. Vivino wrenched free and lunged toward the TV, screaming, "Gimme that tape! Gimme that goddamn tape!"

Mr. Bainbridge swung a fist that caught him in the gut. Jack winced as the man doubled over and sank to one knee.

"I don't think so," Mr. Bainbridge said.

After catching his breath, Mr. Vivino rose to his feet. He was pale and sweaty and looked somehow smaller as he licked his lips and darted quick looks left and right.

"Hey, guys, it's not what it looks like."

"I think it's exactly what it looks like," Mr. Bainbridge said in a voice dripping with scorn. "We're soldiers, Al. Women and children are noncombatants."

This brought a chorus of agreement from the other vets.

Jack realized that they had started off the evening as comrades in arms, good-buddy veterans of foreign wars. That had changed. They were now husbands and fathers, and they were sickened and angry.

"And you know what?" Mr. Bainbridge said, getting in Vivino's face. "You're not going home tonight. 'Cause if you do, you'll probably take it out on Cathy. So Evelyn and I are going over, and we'll stay there all night if we have to."

Mr. Bishop stepped forward. "I cannot believe this, Al. I can*not* believe it!"

"Hey, you know how it is."

Mr. Bishop reddened. "I know no such thing. I'm going to help Cathy get a restraining order against you. And as for that tape, I'm delivering it to dye-fuss first thing tomorrow."

Dye-fuss? Jack thought.

Then he got it: DYFS—Division of Youth and Family Services. They dealt with cases of child abuse.

"No!" Mr. Vivino wailed. "You can't do this!"

Jack had heard enough. He rose, brushed off his knees, then his hands.

What was that expression? *My work here is done.*

He felt strange. He hadn't known if his plan would work, but he'd expected to feel happy and satisfied if it had.

Well, it had worked out perfectly: Mr. Vivino's abuse had been exposed and his name was mud. He wouldn't be beating on Sally and her mom anymore.

So why didn't he feel great?

7

Jack's mind was elsewhere as he pulled his bike out from beside USED. He was just starting up Quakerton Road when he was startled by a screech of tires. He looked up and saw the grille of a Bentley inches from his front wheel.

The window rolled down and a familiar voice spoke from within.

"You almost dented my car."

Jack walked his bike to the window. "Sorry, Mister Drexler."

His sharp-featured face floated into view. "Even worse, if you'd broken a leg I'd have to find a new groundskeeper."

Groundskeeper . . . was that what he was?

"Wouldn't want to put you to extra trouble."

"Speaking of groundskeeping, I'm awaiting an invoice for your services."

"Invoice . . . is that like a bill?"

The thin lips curved ever so slightly upward. "Very much like a bill. In fact, exactly like a bill."

"Oh. Okay."

Jack had never billed anyone in his life, but he was sure his father would know what to do.

The window rose and the car glided away.

As Jack watched it go he realized the Lodge was empty now—or at least would be for a while.

And it had no alarm system.

And the pyramid was probably back in its spot on the mantel.

And his luck had been running high today.

Still, he hesitated. A big step. Sneaking into the Lodge meant breaking the law, risking arrest. But he and Weezy had as much right to that pyramid as anyone—maybe more. And maybe getting it back would take Weezy off the emotional roller coaster she was riding. If nothing else, she'd stop talking about it. That would be a relief.

Do it, he thought.

If not now, when? He was feeling nearly invincible tonight.

Now . . . it had to be now.

He headed back to USED for the lock-pick kit.

8

Thunder rumbled as they approached the rear of the Lodge.

"Why are we walking?" Eddie whined. "That's why God gave us bikes—so we don't have to walk."

"Did it ever occur to you," Weezy said, "that we can't leave three bikes outside."

"Oh, yeah. Duh on me."

Jack led the way. He'd been here only a little while ago to pick the lock. He hadn't said anything about that because he didn't want word of that particular skill getting around. He could have sneaked in and found the pyramid on his own—if it was still here—but he'd made a deal with Weezy.

. . . we'll do it together . . .

"See?" he said. "All the lights are off and the car's gone."

"But how do we get in?"

"I don't know." He pointed to the back door. "Maybe they forgot to lock up. You heard Mister Drexler: No alarm system because why would anyone want to rob the place? Didn't seem to worry much about a break-in. Try the door."

Weezy grabbed the knob, twisted, and the door swung inward.

"What?"

Jack looked first at Eddie, then Weezy. He couldn't make out their faces in the darkness.

Then lightning flashed. Instinctively he jumped, but the flash illuminated their uncertain expressions.

"Hey," he said as thunder followed. "We're here. We've

come this far. The least we should do is take a quick look to see if the pyramid's inside."

"Okay," Weezy said, her voice tight. "Let's do it."

Jack turned to Eddie. "You with us?"

A long pause, then, "Okay, as long as you can guarantee we're not gonna see Gargamel in the white suit."

"Mister Drexler?" Jack laughed. "I can pretty much guarantee it."

"All right. But if I go in with you guys, it's just for a look because, I mean, I don't know *any* kid who's been inside the Lodge."

"But you can't blab about it," Weezy said. "This isn't legal. You could get us all in trouble."

"I won't say a word. Just want to go inside so I can say—just to myself and nobody else, okay?—that I've been inside. But when it comes time to snatch back your baby pyramid, I'm outta here. Don't want anything to do with that."

"Fine. Whatever. Let's get in and get out and get home."

Jack stepped inside and turned on the flashlight from USED. He held the door for Weezy and Eddy, then closed it behind them. The other two each had flashlights of their own and turned them on.

"Keep the beams toward the floor," Jack said. "We don't want anyone spotting the light." Lightning lit the windows as he started into the kitchen.

"That's it," Eddie said. "I'm done."

Jack turned to him. "What?"

"I'm here, I'm inside, that's all I wanted. You two can go get your pyramid. I'm history. See you at home."

With that he turned and slipped out the back door. It had started to rain.

Weezy seemed to waver, then said, "Let's go."

He led her to the front room where he swept his flash beam across the mantel, stopping when it found the pyramid.

Lightning lit the room as he heard Weezy gasp.

"They put it back! It's here! It's really here!"

"It sure is." When Weezy didn't move, just stood there staring, he added, "Go ahead. Take it. It's yours."

She handed him her flashlight, and he stuck it in his back pocket. Then he watched as she took the pyramid from the mantel and cradled it in her arms like a baby. She gazed down at it a moment, then looked up at Jack. Were those tears in her eyes?

"I can't believe it," she said in a hushed tone that seemed to teeter on the edge of a sob. "It's back . . . I've got it back. And they're never taking it away again."

Fine with Jack. The sooner they were out of the Lodge, the better.

"Let's go then."

Feeling jubilant, he trained his flash beam on the floor and led Weezy toward the back door. They'd done it. No doubt about it—today was his day.

But as they were stepping into the kitchen, light flashed through the windows. But not lightning this time—headlights, swinging around to the rear of the Lodge.

"Oh no!" Weezy cried as a car pulled up to the back door. "Someone's here!"

Jack dashed to a window and peeked out. His knees wobbled when he saw the Bentley.

Mr. Drexler was back!

As Eggers stepped out into the rain, Jack rushed back to Weezy.

"We've got to get out of here!"

He grabbed her arm and pulled her back to the front room where he found the door locked. No time to pick the double-key dead bolt.

Trapped!

"Jack!" Weezy wailed. "What do we do?"

Only one option.

"Hide!"

He led her to the stairs but decided against the second floor. That might be just where Eggers was headed. He tugged on the door to the basement Weezy had opened the other day. Mr. Drexler had mentioned it was used as a storage area.

"In here! Quick!"

They stepped onto a small landing and closed the door behind them. Weezy huddled against him. He could feel her trembling.

"I'm scared, Jack."

So was Jack, but he didn't say so.

"We'll be okay." He was trying very hard to believe that. "What's the worst that could happen? We're just trespassing. We're not vandals. We haven't hurt anything. And we haven't left yet, so no one can accuse us of stealing." He forced a soft laugh. "We'll just be grounded for life."

She squeezed his arm. "Don't you understand? We're not dealing with regular folks. This is the Septimus Order. They make their own rules."

Jack heard the back door open. He recognized Eggers's voice, but he seemed to be speaking in German. No . . . it sounded like he was *cursing* in German.

Jack put his lips close to Weezy's ear. "Maybe we'd be better off at the bottom of the steps."

He turned on the flashlight and together they tiptoed

down to the basement. Once they reached the floor he swept the beam around the big, windowless space and found it full of old furniture. He couldn't help thinking how Mr. Rosen would have a field day down here.

"What do you mean about the Order making its own rules? How do you know?"

"I've read a lot. You know that. No one's actually come out and said anything, but they've hinted that the Septimus Order does not play nice with people who get in their way or ask too many questions."

"What's that mean?"

"Troublemakers simply aren't seen anymore. They go away. They disappear."

A chill rippled over Jack's skin, but he shook it off. Mr. Drexler wouldn't . . .

He realized he really didn't know what Mr. Drexler would do. He was soft-spoken and mannerly, but he also seemed cold and unfeeling. He was the Order's "actuator." He made things happen. If he saw Jack and Weezy as a threat, would he make them disappear?

He shook off another chill. That sounded crazy. Still . . . he didn't want to find out.

Just then, stomping footsteps rattled the ceiling. Eggers—or someone else up there—was mad about something. With a start Jack realized what it was.

"He might think someone's inside," he whispered.

Weezy gripped his arm. "Why?"

"The back door was unlocked. And maybe he's noticed the pyramid's gone."

Weezy's grip tightened. "What if he searches down here?"

Just what Jack was thinking.

"Let's find a hiding place."

He pulled Weezy's flashlight from his back pocket and handed it to her. Together they started walking the narrow lanes between the stacks of furniture, searching for a secluded spot. Jack found a big armoire and pulled open the doors. He flashed his light around the empty interior.

"No sign of Narnia," he said.

"I *wish*."

He glanced at her. "Big enough for two."

She shook her head. "I couldn't stay in there. It's too . . ."

"I thought Eddie was the claustrophobic one."

"He is. But hiding in there in a dark cellar in the Lodge of all places . . . I don't think I can. I need to be someplace where I can hear and see."

Urgency propelled Jack as he flashed his beam around. Behind the armoire sat a low, wide, sturdy-looking table with what appeared to be Chinese lettering along its edges. It was backed against a leather couch and its other side rested against the rear of a bureau, leaving only one side open.

He focused his beam on the space beneath. "How about under there? If we scrunch up way toward the rear we should be really hard to find."

Weezy stared for a heartbeat or two, then nodded.

"Okay. But you first."

Swell.

But he understood: ladies first—unless there might be spiders.

He knelt and did a quick inspection. No black widows hanging out, just a thick layer of dust and some cobwebs. He crawled under, and Weezy followed. Jack turned out his flashlight and Weezy did the same. Side by side, with the pyramid sitting between them, they crouched in the cramped, cool darkness.

Weezy whispered, "How will we know—?"

The lights came on.

Weezy grabbed his hand and squeezed.

9

They waited. And waited. It was becoming excruciating—physically as well as emotionally.

Physically because Weezy was squeezing his hand so hard his fingers were going numb. Emotionally because the light had come on and stayed on and no one had come downstairs.

Was Eggers or Mr. Drexler standing at the top and listening? Jack wanted to whisper to Weezy to ease up on his hand but didn't dare. Didn't want even to breathe, but had no choice in that.

Finally it came: footsteps on the stairs.

Someone with a heavy tread—had to be Eggers—stomped down to the basement and began stalking its aisles. Weezy squeezed even harder as the footsteps approached. Jack saw black shoes and black pants cuffs appear and stop right in front of their table.

Eggers. Mr. Drexler was wearing his usual white suit when Jack had last seen him . . . not quite an hour ago.

Not daring to move his head, Jack glanced at Weezy out of the corner of his eye. Her face was ashen and her eyes were squeezed shut. She wasn't breathing. But then, neither was Jack. He could feel the sweat gathering in his armpits.

The shoes moved on but Jack didn't dare let out the breath he'd been holding, not until they'd faded to the other side of the room. And then he let it out really, really slowly. He noticed Weezy doing the same. She looked at him with a terrified expression.

Did she really think the Order would harm them if they were found here?

Apparently so.

Finally, after what seemed like an eternity, the footsteps headed back upstairs. The light went out and the door slammed.

Jack felt Weezy relax and begin to move. He quickly touched her face in the dark, found her lips, and put a finger against them. When he felt her nod that she understood, he began extricating his hand from hers. That done, he put his lips against her ear and spoke in the softest voice possible.

"Don't speak, don't move."

She nodded again.

After another eternity—probably ten minutes—he dared a whisper.

"Okay. I guess he's really gone."

He felt her stiffen. "What do you mean?"

"Well, if it had been me, I would have turned out the light and closed the door from the inside. Then I would have waited on the landing and listened to see if anyone moved down here."

She let out a breath. "I'm glad whoever that was isn't like you. But what do we do now?"

"We wait."

"How long? How will we know when he goes?"

Jack almost said, *You mean,* if *he goes,* but thought better of it.

"We'll be real quiet and listen for the back door slamming."

He didn't know if that was possible. These walls were thick—he could barely hear the thunder. He kept that to himself. She was already scared enough.

10

Jack guessed that twenty minutes more had passed. If not for the tense circumstances, it might have been nice being squeezed next to Weezy like this.

He'd heard more footsteps on the other side of the ceiling, and then, maybe ten minutes ago, a sound like the back door slamming. After that, all sounds ceased. He hadn't heard the car start, but that didn't mean anything, considering what lay between them and the rear driveway. Only one thing to do.

He turned on his flashlight.

"Wait here. I'm going to check upstairs."

"No, Jack. He could still be up there."

"Yeah, he could. But we can't stay here forever." He crawled out from under the table and reached a hand toward her. "Might as well come out."

She turned on her flashlight and shook her head. "I'll stay here till you come back."

"Okay. I'll put the lights on when I pass the switch."

"Do you think you should?"

He shrugged. "No windows down here, so no one outside's gonna notice. Neither will anyone up there. Be back in a few minutes."

I hope.

He found the light switch at the top of the stairs, but didn't flip it on. Not yet. He needed to peek onto the first floor before that.

He bent until his line of sight was at floor level. No light filtered beneath the door. Dark out there.

Good.

Grasping the knob, he twisted it as slowly as he could until it would turn no more. Then, praying the hinges wouldn't squeak, he began to push the door open—also slowly—until the edge cleared the frame.

Still no sign of light, so—

He jumped as a flickering flash of white lit up an area to his left, quickly followed by a roar of thunder. He turned on the basement lights before slipping out the door and easing it closed behind him. Bad enough leaving Weezy alone and afraid down there; at least she wouldn't be in the dark.

He looked around. No sign of life or man-made light here on the first floor, although the lightning flashes were frequent. Rain blew in torrents against the windows. The storm had hit full force.

But an empty first floor didn't guarantee an empty second. He peered up the dark stairwell. No noise or light from up there either.

He took off his sneakers and glided in his socks to the back door. He sagged with relief when he saw no sign of the Bentley.

Mr. Drexler and Eggers had gone.

But just to be sure . . . just to be absolutely sure, Jack eased up the steps and made a quick, nerve-wracking pass through the second floor. As he wandered the lightning-strobed hallway, a parade of horror film scenes—especially someone or something jumping out of a darkened doorway—flickered through his mind. But his search came up empty—just the way he'd hoped.

No longer afraid of making noise, he hurried down to the first floor and opened the basement door.

"Hey, Weez!" he called. "All clear!"

She didn't answer.

"Weez?"

Still no answer.

Oh, jeez. Oh, no.

With his blood feeling as if it were congealing in his veins, he slipped back into his sneakers and crept down to the brightly lit basement.

"Weez?"

He ran to the table where they'd hidden and looked under it. He found her flashlight and the pyramid, but not a trace of her.

"Oh, God—Weez!"

"I'm right here," said a voice behind him.

He whirled and saw her head sticking out from under the table opposite theirs.

"Don't do that to me!"

She puzzled. "I didn't do anything." She crawled out, dusting off her hands. When she regained her feet she pointed to the space she'd just left. "Look what I found."

Jack dropped to his knees and saw a thick semicircle of braided steel protruding from the concrete.

"What is it?"

"I noticed it when I was waiting for you. It looks like a handle."

He looked up at her. "A handle? What—?"

"Help me move the table."

He rose and together they moved it off the spot and down the aisle. Once the area was clear, Jack saw a rectangular groove in the floor. He brushed and blew the dust out of the seam on the far side from the handle and found sunken hinges. Pretty clear what they had here.

"A trapdoor."

Weezy nodded. "Just what I thought. Especially when I tapped on it."

Jack rapped his knuckles on the surface and heard a deep, hollow, gonging sound.

"Steel."

"Yes," Weezy said, her voice vibrating with excitement. "Made to look like concrete."

Jack bent for a closer look. Based on the amount of dust and dirty sand in the grooves, the trapdoor or whatever it was hadn't been opened for a long time.

He grabbed the ring and tugged. The door wouldn't budge. He put his back into it with the same result.

"Give me a hand."

Weezy added her strength to the pull but to no avail.

"I think it's locked," she said.

Jack inspected the dirty surface. "If so, it must be from the other side, because there's no keyhole."

"We've *got* to get it open, Jack. It's obviously a secret compartment that's been locked for who knows how long. Just think what could be hidden inside. Ancient books, infernal devices, *secrets*!"

Jack stared at her shining eyes, her intent expression. "Okay . . . how?"

"I don't know, but—hey, here's something."

She began brushing the dirt from a shallow depression in the trapdoor surface. Only it wasn't so shallow. The dirt kept coming. And as she brushed it free, the edges of the depression became visible.

"Jack, it's got six sides! And it tapers down to a point, I think!"

Her hands began to shake, so Jack lent his to the task and . . .

"You're right . . . the same size and shape as . . . you think . . . ?"

Weezy was already under the other table, grabbing the pyramid.

"Yes! It'll fit! It has to!"

Jack brushed-blew out the remaining debris from the hexagonal depression and took the pyramid from her. He placed it point-down into the cavity and leaned back.

"Near perfect fit."

"Jack . . ." He could barely hear her. "I think it's the key."

The top three-quarters of the pyramid were settled into the opening, leaving the hexagonal base protruding. Jack leaned closer and noticed a circular groove running around the cavity, like it was set in the end of a cylinder.

"I think you're right."

He gripped the base and tried to rotate it, but it wouldn't budge—clockwise or counterclockwise, no luck, not even with Weezy's help.

"It's jammed." He looked around. "Maybe we'd better go. We're stretching our luck by staying here and—"

"Are you kidding?" she said, her voice jumping an octave. "They're gone, right?"

"Well, yeah."

"Then we're not going anywhere until we get that door open."

He realized argument was futile.

"Okay, but—"

"Wait a minute," she said, grabbing a flashlight. "I thought I saw something inside when I was cleaning it out." She removed the pyramid and trained the beam on the cavity. The light wavered in her trembling hand as it revealed little rough spots on each of its six facets. "Don't those look familiar?"

Jack leaned closer and immediately recognized them.

"The symbols on the pyramid. So it *does* belong in there."

"Right, but maybe it's got to be in there a certain way—with the glyphs matched up."

So that was what they did: Matched up the glyphs on the six sides of the pyramid with those on the facets of the cavity.

But when Jack tried it again it still wouldn't turn.

"It's got to!" Weezy cried, her tone frantic. "It's jammed!"

She rose and stomped on the base of the pyramid with a sneakered foot.

"Hey!" Jack said as she kept kicking it. "What are you doing?"

"This is what my dad does when something is jammed. He whacks it. So . . ."

Another kick or two and then she knelt beside him and they both tried rotating the pyramid.

It budged counterclockwise.

"Did you feel it?" Weezy cried.

Jack nodded and increased his efforts. He felt another budge. And then another. He and Weezy were grunting, their breath rasping though their teeth.

With a *crunch,* something broke free within the mechanism and the pyramid made a quick quarter turn. And then another quarter. And after that it made steady progress until it completed a full turn.

"I think that does it," Jack said. "What now? Open it?"

Weezy nodded, eyes shining. "Are you kidding?"

Jack thought about the mound, and all the trouble digging into that had caused. And now this. What secrets had the Order hidden behind the trapdoor that only it, as possessor of the pyramid, could open?

Jack wasn't sure he wanted to know. He was also sure that no way could he walk away from this door without seeing what lay behind it.

"Okay. On my count of three." Together they grabbed the ring handle. "One . . . two . . . *three*!"

11

"I can't believe it."

Jack didn't know how long they'd stood in silence and stared at the dark hole before Weezy spoke.

He sighed. "Yeah. All that crazy lock business for a hole in the ground." He squatted for a closer look at the rectangle of empty blackness. "Or maybe not."

He grabbed one of the flashlights and aimed its beam into the opening. About ten feet down he saw a flat expanse of what looked like wet stone and mud. Weezy was at his side, craning her neck for a look.

"Looks like a subcellar," she said. "But no stairs."

Still beaming his flashlight into the opening, Jack moved around to the other side and found something.

"Hey. Steps. Sort of."

A stone wall sat under Weezy's side. Deep horizontal grooves had been cut into the surface, allowing it to function as a ladder of sorts.

"I'm going down for a look," Jack said.

"You think it's safe?"

He looked at her. "You mean, is there anyone or anything down there? You saw that door. It hasn't been opened for ages."

She shrugged. "I guess you're right. It's just that it's so . . . dark."

He smiled and held up the flashlight. "That's why we have these."

He wasn't sure why he wanted to descend into the space. Maybe simply because it was there. Or maybe because he didn't think he'd ever get another chance like this.

Whatever the reason, he felt a tug from the darkness.

He stuck the flashlight in his back pocket and eased himself over the edge until his sneaker found one of the grooves. Then it was almost like climbing a ladder.

When he reached the bottom his sneakers splashed a little. More water down here than he'd originally thought. He was glad he'd worn his old Converses.

"See anything?"

Weezy knelt at the edge of the opening, staring down at him. He glanced around: stone wall in front of him, stone wall behind, and blackness left and right.

"Looks like I'm in a passage of some sort."

Pulling out the flashlight, he turned it on and moved to his right. He didn't go far before he ran into a third stone wall. This was cracked and flaky, with water seeping around its edges and through the cracks.

He closed his eyes and oriented himself within the Lodge and realized he was below and beyond its west wall. Which put this wall right near the bank of the lake. He gauged that it would normally sit just above surface level. But now, with the lake so high, it had to be underwater. This was the lake seeping through.

He backtracked and found Weezy where he'd left her, peering down at him.

"Empty dead end back there. I'll check this way."

He'd walked perhaps twenty feet when his beam picked out something leaning against a wall. It took him a moment to recognize its shape, and when he did, he knew he had to show Weezy.

He made his way back to the shaft of light shining from the Lodge's basement.

"Weez! I found something!"

"What? A book, a scroll? What?"

"You've got to see it to believe it. Trust me."

She hesitated barely a second. "I do." She held out her flashlight. "Catch."

He did just that, then watched her scamper down the wall like she'd done it a thousand times.

"You're pretty good at that."

She smiled. "Queen of the monkey bars—remember?"

He nodded. She'd been pretty limber and agile as a kid. A lot of the boys had been unable to keep up with her.

She took her flashlight and turned it on.

"Now. Where's this thing I've got to see?"

"Follow me."

Aiming his light far ahead, he led her down the passage. His beam soon found the object.

"There. How soon can you figure out what it is?"

Jack had been practically on top of it before he recognized it.

Weezy slowed her pace, then stopped a few feet from it.

"It looks like the Septimus seal."

"Right. It's the sigil. But I've never seen one like this."

All the others had been either sculpted or molded in relief on a circular base. This was just the figure itself—six feet high, Jack guessed—and not made of the usual stone or plaster.

Weezy stepped forward and ran a finger over its dust-laden surface.

"It feels like . . ."

Jack did the same and knew what she was thinking. Under the grime the surface was a smooth, shiny black.

Her voice was hushed with awe. "The same material as our pyramid!" She ran her fingers over the rough edges at one of the corners. "But the border is all broken off."

"All except one section up top." Jack ran his flash beam over it and immediately recognized the figures carved into the surviving section. "Hey, Weez—"

"I see. The same seven glyphs as on the pyramid—what do they mean? What do they spell? And why aren't they on the other sigils, like the one over the front door?"

"Lots of good questions, Weez. And I've got a few more. Like, what was written on the other sections? And why does Mister Drexler have one of the glyphs on his cane?"

She looked at him. "The glyphs here and on the locking mechanism on that door don't leave much question as to the true owner of the pyramid."

He sighed and gave a reluctant nod. "Yeah. The Lodge."

Too bad.

"You don't really think I'm leaving it here, do you? No way. Finders keepers, and I found it." Her expression turned fierce as her voice rose. "I am never, *ever* giving it up again!"

"Okay, but—"

"What is this place, anyway?" she said as she flashed her light around—her mood had done a complete about-face. It seemed to change direction like her flash beam. "I can't believe they built all this just to store this one broken-down sigil. I—" She stopped when her beam picked up a dark rectangle in the wall farther down on the left side of the passage. "Doesn't that look like . . . ?"

"Yeah," Jack said, moving toward it. "A doorway. Let's see."

Yes, a doorway in the stone wall, with no door. And a little to its right, another opening, smaller, square, chest high.

"This almost looks like a window."

"But that's crazy," Weezy said. "Who'd put a window underground?"

Jack shone his beam within and saw more walls and what looked like another doorway. He stepped inside and found a partially collapsed stone ceiling. Rocky debris littered the space. Through the second doorway lay another space, this one even more choked with debris.

"You know . . . ," Weezy said, close behind him, "this almost looks like a house."

"Exactly what I was thinking. A very small house, but a house."

They returned to the passageway and moved on. They passed a rock-and-dirt-choked area where something appeared to have collapsed. And then on the right, another doorway leading into what looked like another little house.

And farther along they came to a wider passage crossing theirs. Jack positioned himself at the center of the intersection and turned in a full circle, beaming his flash in all directions.

Back the way they had come he could see the shaft of light from the trapdoor opening, but he was sure they'd progressed beyond the walls of the Lodge. Down the three other paths he found darkness and the hint of other doorways and windows.

"Ohmygod," Weezy said as she turned with him. "You know what this is?"

"It . . . it looks like a town."

"Exactly! Jack, we've discovered a buried town!"

"Who would bury a town?"

"It's not so much buried as built over. It happens all the time. Look at the ancient city of Troy. Archeologists think there are eight cities on that site, one built over another time and time again. It's a layer cake. And York, England, is built over a Roman town, and sections of Rome and London are built over previous towns and cities."

Jack looked around. "So you think we're in one of those lost towns of the Pines you're always talking about?"

"Yes and no. I think this is an ancient, early settlement. Maybe these people built the megalith pyramid out in the Pines. Somewhere along the way, the original Quakerton—what we call Old Town—was built over it." She started jumping up and down in a sort of Snoopy happy dance. "This is amazing! *Amazing!* It's part of the Secret History!"

Jack could see how it could have been built over—the passages were all roofed with stone.

"Well, if these used to be their streets, why did they cover them? I mean, it's like an ancient mall."

"Maybe they were hiding from someone or something."

"Like what?"

Weezy shrugged. "How should I know?"

"I thought you knew all this stuff."

"In everything I've read about the Pines, lost towns were mentioned, but never anything like this. This wasn't even hinted at. Not once. Oh, God, this is *so* great!"

Then they stood in silence a moment, each turning and beaming light down the passages.

"Well," Jack said finally, letting his light come to rest on Weezy. "What do you want to do?"

"I want to explore—I really do. We may never get another chance." She chewed her lip. "But I have this awful, terrible fear . . ."

"Of what?"

"That someone is going to come down to the basement, see the door open, and close it."

Jack's stomach lurched. He looked back along their original passage and was reassured by the warm glow shining from the ceiling.

"You had to say that? You *had* to say that? Now you've got me thinking about it."

"Sorry. It's just that it's my worst nightmare."

"Well, thanks, because now you've just made it mine. Let's get out of here."

Before Weezy could reply, Jack heard a high-pitched sound. He touched her arm.

"You hear that?"

She cocked her head and stood statue still for a heartbeat or two as the sound rose and fell in pitch and volume. She closed her eyes and looked like she was in a trance.

"That's what I heard on the tour. I think it's a voice."

Now that she mentioned it, it did sound something like a voice.

Suddenly she gasped as her eyes flew open.

"Jack, it's a child!"

12

After listening awhile longer, concentrating with everything he had, Jack had to agree. It wasn't a cat.

"Yeah. It does sound sort of like a kid." A small, very scared kid. "Cody!"

"Oh, no!" Weezy said. "You think Drexler kidnapped him and locked him down here?"

As weird and creepy as Mr. Drexler was, Jack didn't think so.

"Think about it: How would he get him down here? Not through that door we used—we're the first to open that thing in a *long* time."

"Okay. So maybe it wasn't him. But if it's Cody, how did he get down here?"

"I don't know. Maybe he fell in somewhere and couldn't get out. We'll worry about that later." He cupped his hands around his mouth and shouted, *"Cody!"*

They stood statue still and silent, waiting. And then it came . . . faint, faraway, even higher pitched, but unmistakable.

"Hello? Is someone there? Hello?"

Jack wanted to cheer. He was alive! Cody was alive, and they'd found him!

"We hear you, Cody!" Jack called. "We're coming to get you! Just keep talking!"

But he didn't keep talking. He started crying, and the relief and terror in the sound tore at Jack.

He grabbed Weezy's arm. "Let's go."

But she held back, looking over her shoulder. Jack followed her gaze and saw the shaft of light from the trapdoor. He remembered her fear of someone closing it and locking them down here.

. . . it's my worst nightmare . . .

Yeah, but they couldn't leave Cody. Not after what he'd already been through.

Handing her his flashlight, he said, "Wait here."

He ran back toward the trapdoor. Along the way he encountered water sooner than expected. It was spreading and deepening, and had reached all the way to the first doorway now. At the base of the trapdoor ladder it was ankle deep and *cold* as it filled his sneakers.

That stone barrier at the other end must have sprung more leaks, or the existing ones had enlarged.

He rushed up the ladder to the cellar and checked beneath the trapdoor. The pyramid had fallen out when they'd lifted the door. He pulled a chair over to the opening, then lifted the door and wedged it against it. Then he reinserted the pyramid in the cavity and began turning. It took only a fraction of the effort he'd needed to open it.

As he turned he watched three latches—top, bottom, and side—slide out. He'd thought there was only one. Man, they sure must have wanted to keep people out of that passage down there.

And then a thought struck: Or had they wanted to keep something down there from coming up?

Don't go there, he told himself.

He pulled the pyramid from the cavity, pushed the door back, and then checked out his handiwork: With the latches locked out, the door couldn't close.

And without the pyramid—which Jack was going to take with him—no way anyone could retract the latches.

Unless, of course, they had another pyramid.

Don't go there either, he thought.

He slipped through the doorway and down the ladder to the passage—

—where the water was now about an inch *above* his ankles.

Not good. That barrier had to be leaking pretty badly. If it ever gave way . . .

And especially don't go there.

They had to find Cody and get him out ASAP.

He thought about going for help, but that could take a while. How long for the two of them to find Cody? Five minutes tops. And another five to get him back to the ladder. The poor kid had waited long enough.

He splashed back to Weezy and showed her the pyramid.

"No one can lock us down here now." He placed it in the center of the intersection. "And this will mark the spot we need to come back to."

"Where are you?" cried a small, faraway voice. *"Are you still there?"*

"We're coming, Cody!" Jack called. "Stay right where you are and keep yelling 'hello.' We'll find you." He looked at Weezy. "Okay. Let's go get him."

Weezy nodded and pointed to their left. "I think he's that way."

Jack agreed, so they set off in that direction.

They'd speed-walked maybe a hundred feet when they came to another intersection, this one a T with the leg running to their right. Cody's voice seemed to be coming down the leg.

Jack pointed and started in that direction, then stopped.

He looked back the way they'd come and saw only darkness.

"Hey, we could get lost."

"I don't get lost," Weezy said. "And you won't as long as you stay with me."

True. Weezy never got lost. She'd wander all through the Pines and always find her way back. But this was different.

"You're sure? This isn't like being in the Barrens. You can't see the sky. No sun or stars to guide you. There's not even any light."

She tapped her forehead. "I don't know how it works, but it's all up here. I always remember the paths I take. I can always go back the way I came."

That wasn't all she remembered. Her photographic memory didn't let her forget anything she'd ever read. He envied her that.

"Okay. I'm counting on you."

They hurried on, their progress slowed by a pile of rocks and dirt where the ceiling had given way. They picked their way over that, then continued on.

"I'm worried about something else," Weezy said. "What if it's not Cody?"

"How can it be anyone else? He's the only kid who's disappeared."

"But what if it's not a kid? What if it's some*thing* else?"

"Oh, jeez. You're not going to start, are you? What else could it be?"

"Well, we know there's something out in the Pines, something that chases people—we know that from personal experience."

"Okay, yeah. But that was a bear."

"You're calling it a bear, but we never got a clear look at it."

"It was a *bear*, Weez."

Had to be.

"But what if it was something else . . . something with the power to lure you to it by sounding like a frightened child?"

"Weez, it's *speaking* to us. Listen."

Somewhere up ahead a child's voice was repeating, "Hello? . . . Hello . . . Hello?"

"I know, I know. I just . . ."

They came to another four-way intersection and Weezy stopped, turning in a circle.

"You know what?" she said.

Jack wasn't sure he wanted to hear this.

"What?"

"Remember the black cube the pyramid came in, and how it had that pattern of crisscrossing lines etched on its inside?"

"Sure. You made a tracing."

"Well, I've always wondered what they represented. I mean they weren't random. They formed a sort of grid. I'm beginning to believe it was a street map."

"Of this place?"

She nodded. "Yeah. I'm not sure yet, but—hey!" She jumped as if she'd been bitten on the foot. "What—?"

Jack aimed his flashlight down and saw water swirling around their sneakers. He hadn't noticed because his feet were already wet.

"This is not good," he said. "This is not good at all."

"What's going on?"

"The lake . . . it's seeping through."

Her voice rose an octave. "You call this *seeping*?"

"Okay. It's *breaking* through."

"But Jack, have you noticed? We've been on a slight

incline. That means the water's already lots deeper back where we came from."

"Hello?" came the little voice. *"Are you still there?"*

"We're coming, Cody!" Jack called, then turned to Weezy. "We'd better hurry."

She said, "Thank you, Captain Obvious," but her tone didn't carry its usual edge.

She was worried. So was Jack.

Flashing their lights ahead of them, they broke into a trot. Recurrent areas of debris where the roof had collapsed slowed them, but they kept going.

They arrived at an intersection where the voice seemed to be coming more from their right, so they veered that way. But after maybe twenty feet . . .

"Eew!" Weezy said. "What's that smell?"

Together they skidded to a halt as a rotten odor rammed into his nostrils. They each clapped a hand over nose and mouth. Not the same as the thing in the Pines last night.

"It smells like something died," he said.

Weezy took a tentative step forward and pointed to a doorway on their left.

"I . . . I think it's coming from in there." She looked at Jack. "Go see what it is."

Jack's first instinct was to ask her why *she* didn't go see, but he bit it back. They needed to know.

If Cody had wound up in the lost town, then something else might have as well. Whatever was stinking up the place probably hadn't been able to get out and had starved to death. Cody was looking at the same fate if they didn't get him out.

Jack shone his light through the doorway as he inched up to it, but saw nothing but bare floor and walls. When he reached it the smell hit him like a punch in the face. Holding his nose wasn't good enough—-he could *taste* the odor, and it made him gag.

Steeling himself he stepped inside and flashed his beam left—nothing—and right—

Jack stood frozen in shock at the mound of bones piled in the corner—old bones and new bones, a couple with bits of meat still clinging to them, animal bones and human bones, and oh yeah he was sure they were human because he'd seen pictures and had inspected the life-size plastic skeleton in the school's biology lab and who could mistake those two skulls up front there for anything but human and they had tooth gouges and holes in the top just like the skull they'd found in the pyramid cage in the Pines.

13

Jack reeled backward, bumping into Weezy and almost knocking her down.

"Jack! What—?"

"Bones!" he gasped, trying to catch his breath. "A hundred—a million of them! Eaten—something's killing animals and people and bringing them down here to eat!"

Marcie Kurek's name flashed through his brain. Could one of those skulls be hers?

"People?" Weezy stepped back and splashed into a puddle. "Oh, no!"

The water had followed them.

"Hello?" came Cody's voice, louder now that they were closer, and from somewhere to their right, just on the far side of a high mound of debris. *"Are you still coming?"*

Jack opened his mouth to reply, then recalled what Weezy had said about something luring people with the sound of a child. He envisioned an angler fish, dangling its wiggly lure right outside its huge, sharp-toothed mouth, drawing unsuspecting prey closer and closer until . . .

"Cody!" he called. "What's your last name?"

"Bockman! Where are you?"

Jack glanced at Weezy and saw that she looked as relieved as he felt.

"Keep talking, Cody!" he shouted.

They picked their way over the pile of rocks and dirt and came upon a doorway where a little boy, dirty and disheveled with tear-streaked cheeks, stood blinking in their flash beams. He looked different from the last time Jack had seen him. His blond hair was matted, his face pale, his eyes sunken, but no doubt about it: This was Cody Bockman.

"Who-who are you?" he sobbed, then ducked back inside.

Jack realized that with their beams directed in his face, all the kid could see was their lights. Jack lowered his beam as he and Weezy slipped through the doorway.

"Hey, Code. It's me—Jack!"

"Jack?" He ran forward. "Jack?"

He threw his arms around Jack's legs and clutched him like a drowning sailor.

It stank inside, but nothing like the bone room back down the passage. He swept the beam around and saw apple cores and scraps of food—plus his Frisbee, and Eddie's *Star Trek* phasers, and the pink beach ball he'd seen in the Vivinos' yard, and lots of other toys and stuff.

What was going on here?

"You're really going to take me home?"

Weezy knelt before him.

"Absolutely."

He threw his arms around her and sobbed.

"It's okay, it's okay," Weezy said soothingly, showing a side Jack had never seen. "We're going to take you back to your folks."

"Will it let you?"

Jack's gut instantly wound into a Gordian knot.

"'It'?"

"The thing that took me." He began sobbing.

"Oh jeez, what's it look like?"

"I never seen it. All I know is it smells bad. I was riding my bike in the woods and something hit me and I woke up here."

"But how have you survived without food or water or—"

"It brings me food and water. Sometimes fruit, sometimes stuff that's old and don't taste good."

Jack was having difficulty buying this. "And you've never *seen* it?"

"It's dark! I can't see in the dark!"

Right. Dumb question. But obviously whatever took him had no problem with darkness.

Jack flicked his beam over to the toys.

"How'd these get here?"

"It brings them, like it wants me to play with them, but I just want to go ho-ho-home!"

As he started sobbing again, Weezy rose and took him by the hand.

"That's where we're taking you right now." She looked at Jack with a frightened expression. "As fast as we possibly can."

"Even faster," he said, and led the way through the door—

—into water. The whole buried town seemed to be filling with water.

"Better get a real move on," he said, "or we'll be swimming home."

He started to climb the debris mound. "I'll go first, Cody. You stay close behind and I'll help you—"

"Jack!" Weezy said in a harsh whisper. "Listen!"

From somewhere in the distance on the other side of the mound, Jack heard a faraway growl.

"It's coming!" Cody screamed. "It's coming!"

14

The knot in Jack's gut tightened further as the air thickened around him, making it hard to breathe.

Whatever it was that had taken Cody, whatever had eaten the meat off those bones, was approaching along their escape route.

"Quiet, Cody," Weezy whispered as she pulled him away from the mound. "We'll go this way."

"But we came the other way," Jack said, keeping his voice as low as hers as he followed her. "We'll get lost."

"I think I can get us back by another route—by a couple of other routes, actually."

"How?"

She glanced over her shoulder and tapped her head. "The map—it's in here. I think we're under the Klenke house. I'm pretty sure I can get us back to the Lodge. Trust me?"

"I do."

He'd trust her even if he had a choice not to—which he didn't.

But they had to move quickly, and with Cody looking backward all the way, he was going to slow them.

"Hang on, Weez." He pocketed his flash, then gripped Cody's arm and squatted next to him. "Hop on, buddy. You're going to ride."

Without a word Cody climbed onto Jack's back and wrapped his arms around his neck. Hooking his elbows under the boy's knees, Jack straightened and turned to Weezy.

"Okay, you're in charge. Move as fast as you want. I'll keep up."

Flashlight aimed ahead of her, she took off at a cautious trot.

Under the Klenke house . . . the stench Tim had mentioned there . . . the stink from the bone room seeping upward?

He'd worry about that later. Right now he was concerned with the water that had risen to mid-shin level, slowing them.

They'd made a turn and were just skirting a smaller debris mound when an enraged shriek echoed around them.

Feeling Cody tense and take a breath, Jack turned his head and whispered, "Don't make a sound or it'll find us!"

Cody's chest quaked with a repressed sob but the only sound he made was a faint whimper. He tensed again as another shriek split the silence, but he kept mum.

They came to another, larger collapsed area. Climbing over the fallen rocks and dirt wasn't easy with Cody on his back—the kid was solid—but Jack managed.

The water rose to hip level, which was bad because it slowed them even further, but might be good if it meant they were getting closer to their goal. It could also mean the lake was flowing in faster than ever.

Weezy stopped and grabbed his shoulder. She put her lips close to his ear.

"Hear that?"

He listened. Somewhere ahead and to the right, a sound like running water—like a small waterfall emptying into a pond. A good-size hole must have opened up in the stone. Bad news, but it meant they were getting close.

They began moving again, struggling against the cold water. Jack knew he'd be shivering if not for the exertion.

Weezy led them off one passage onto another when a loud splash sounded from the passage they'd just left. A rapid series of smaller splashes followed it.

"It" was coming their way.

Jack pointed to an empty doorway.

"Here!" he whispered. "Light off!"

Weezy turned off her flash as they ducked through a doorway into a watery space as dark as the bottom of a mine shaft. The splashing was growing louder, coming closer.

Jack squatted until the water was up to his neck—*now* he was shivering. He tugged Weezy down next to him, then pulled Cody off his back and positioned him between them.

"Can you hold your breath underwater?" he whispered to the boy. "Like bobs at swim school?" When he felt him nod in return, Jack leaned closer and said to both of them, "When I give the signal, duck under and stay under as long as you can."

He didn't know about the thing's sense of smell, but if it was anything like its vision—what sort of eyes could see in this blackness?—the water could help mask their scent. And that might save their lives.

The splashing grew louder and closer—"it" was pushing hard through the water.

Closer . . .

Louder . . .

Closer . . .

With his lips next to Cody's ear Jack whispered, "Okay now, deep breath and *down*!"

He pushed Weezy down and went under himself with Cody, praying they hadn't ducked too soon. He had decent breath control, and was pretty sure Weezy was okay, but Cody . . . he had no idea how long he could stay under. If he had to come up for air too soon—like when their pursuer was right outside the door—it could mean the end of all of them.

The absolute darkness above the surface seemed even darker below it. The splashing was still audible, but muffled. He felt Cody start to squirm—out of fear rather than need for air, he hoped, because it was too soon. The splashing was only a few feet away. Jack could feel the turbulence of its passing swirl through the door.

Cody was struggling now, pushing upward. Jack didn't want to hold him down any longer, afraid he'd gasp and sputter when he broke the surface and give them away. So he nudged Weezy and all three of them rose.

"A breath and back down!" he whispered in Cody's ear as they broke the surface.

Cody gasped twice, then sank again along with Jack and Weezy.

The splashing outside stopped. Had it heard them? Its own splashing should have drowned out whatever sounds they'd made, but it must have heard *something*—or thought it had. Why else stop?

Jack tried to Obi-Wan it along, thinking, *Move on . . . nothing here . . . move on . . .*

After an eternity during which Cody again began to squirm, it began splashing again—splashing away.

Jack nudged Weezy and the boy to the surface where they gulped air as quietly as they could.

The splashing was growing fainter.

"It's going the way we were headed," Jack whispered.

"We can go another way," Weezy said, her teeth chattering.

"You're sure?"

"Pretty."

Jack would have much preferred "totally" or "absolutely," but he'd take what he could get.

They waited until the splashing died away, then he hoisted Cody onto his back again. Weezy flicked her flashlight, but nothing happened. She shook it but no light.

"Jack?"

Oh no! No-no-no! The possibility of water shorting out the flashlights hadn't even occurred to him. Without light they were doomed.

He grabbed Mr. Rosen's from his pocket. It felt rubberized. As he hit the switch he prayed it had a better seal. The room lit up.

"Thank God!" Weezy said as she snatched it from him and turned it off. "I'm going to turn it on for a second at a time. We'll attract less attention that way."

"Good thinking."

The less attention the better.

With Weezy in the lead, turning on her flash just long enough to give them a direction, they started moving again, retracing their path back to the previous intersection and turning right.

The water had risen above Jack's belt and he was detecting a current—slight, but it slowed their progress more. On the good side, though, if the water was flowing through the crumbling barrier, they need only follow the current to the trapdoor.

The next time Weezy flicked on her flash Jack noticed that the formerly clear water was now muddy. Must have been picking up dirt from the caved-in spots. He saw it swirling their way from around the corner just up ahead to their right. Which meant that was the way to go. He was struggling to catch up to tell Weezy when she angled that way and turned off her light.

Either she'd come to the same conclusion, or was listening to her uncanny sense of direction.

As they rounded the corner a second later he ran into her back.

"What's wrong?" he whispered.

"I can see light up ahead."

Jack pushed ahead for a look. He wanted to shout when he saw the glow seeping from a side passage maybe two hundred feet ahead on the left.

Even though he was ready for it, the current was stronger than he'd expected. Cody was an extra drag, but Jack leaned forward and plowed on. Vaguely silhouetted ahead, Weezy kept the lead, her raised arms stroking the air as if swimming as her lithe body cut through the water—which now swirled around Jack's lower ribs. Good thing he had Cody on his back. The little guy would be completely submerged here.

When they made it to the last intersection, Jack wondered if the little pyramid was still sitting at the center. Doubted it. The current had probably washed it away.

The flow strengthened further as they rounded the last corner. Jack could hear the water rushing in beyond the shaft of light beaming through the trapdoor. He was pretty sure he'd never seen anything so beautiful as that light. He felt a burst of strength and, even though the water was up to his armpits now and Cody seemed heavier than ever, he picked up speed.

He jumped as he felt something brush against a leg. Were fish being washed in from the lake?

Weezy gave up walking and swam ahead with smooth,

strong strokes. It was slow going against the current but eventually she reached the stone ladder and hung there, panting. She had her face turned up toward the doorway when Jack felt a surge of water behind him. Without warning, a deafening shriek of rage filled the passageway and a bolt of pain lanced his scalp as Cody was torn from his back.

Weezy screamed and Jack fell forward, plunging face-first into the cold flow. When he regained his footing and turned, he saw nothing but swirling water.

Cody was gone!

15

"Ohmygod!" Weezy screamed from the ladder. "Ohmygod!"

Jack tried to wade over to her but had to swim through the neck-high water.

"What happened? Did you see it? Where'd he go?"

She pointed a trembling hand toward the darkness of the passage. "Something took him! I heard it screech, and when I looked it had Cody and was diving under the water with him!"

"Flashlight!" Jack said, holding out his hand. "Give!"

Weezy pulled it out of reach. "Are you crazy? You can't go after it! You'll never find it, and if you do it'll kill you!"

But he couldn't just stay here and do nothing.

"What'd it look like?"

She shook her head. "I saw wet black fur and claws and then it was gone. But it was big, Jack. Way bigger than you. That's why you can't go."

"But—"

"Right now the best chance Cody has is if we can go find help and get the police and firemen here."

She was right—Jack knew she was completely right—but he felt as if he was abandoning that little boy.

"All right. But we can't waste a second. Let's see if we can find a phone upstairs."

He wished they'd done that when they'd first heard Cody's voice. But who knew? Who could have imagined this?

"I—" Weezy gasped and pointed to his head. "Jack, you're bleeding!"

Jack touched the back of his head where it hurt and his fingers came away red.

"Must have happened when it snatched Cody." That explained the pain, but he had more important things to worry about. He rinsed his fingers in the swirling water and pointed up. "Come on. Let's go."

As Weezy hauled herself out of the water and began to climb, Jack pulled himself under her and readied to follow. But as he took his first step, something grabbed his trailing leg and pulled him off the ladder and under the surface.

He hadn't had time for a breath. He had no air. He felt clawed paws grip his arms and pull him through the water and away from the light. He choked and fought against inhaling water.

It's trying to drown me!

Suddenly it lifted him from the water and pushed him face-first against the side wall. The slam expelled the water that had been seeping into his throat, and he choked and gasped as he drank air, glorious air.

Though he could hear Weezy's voice screaming his name from a distance, he couldn't see the thing here in the dark with his cheek pressed against the cold rough stone, but he could feel the creature's hot breath on his neck as it growled close behind him. Jack sensed rage and hunger in that sound, and he knew right then he was going to die.

Something like a smooth, thick wet rope snaked around his throat and squeezed. Was it going to strangle him?

Its grip tightened and he shuddered as he felt something warm and rough—it could only be a tongue—squirm against his neck and lap at the blood oozing from his scalp.

The creature stiffened and backed away a few inches, but

didn't release him. After what seemed like a long wait as the water rose toward his chin, the tongue licked him again.

Suddenly the rope uncoiled from his neck and the paws released him. He was free. He heard a splash behind him and spun in the water, but saw nothing. He was alone and that was fine, that was wonderful.

He began kicking and stroking with everything he had toward the light and Weezy's calling voice.

"Jack!" she cried when she saw him. Her words became mixed with sobs. "Hurry, Jack! Hurry!"

He was stroking too hard against the increasing current to speak. Finally he reached the ladder and clutched at it. He looked up and saw Weezy's tear-streaked face staring down at him.

"Oh Jack, I thought you were gone forever!"

So had he. And the thing was, he didn't know why he was alive or how he'd survived. Once the thing had a taste of his blood, it lost interest in him. Was there something wrong with him? With his blood?

Well, if so, he was glad of it. He would have loved to take a few moments here to think about it and catch his breath before climbing, but every second counted for Cody.

His foot found a rung somewhere underwater and he was just starting his climb when he heard a loud crunching *crack!* to his right. He looked and saw a wall of water rushing toward him.

The lake was exploding into the lost town.

Terror ignited a burst of speed in his limbs as he rushed to escape the tsunami, but he'd climbed only halfway through the trapdoor when it hit him. He gasped as the force of it tore his feet from the ladder and dragged his legs along with it. He might have been sucked back into the tor-rent if Weezy hadn't grabbed one of his arms and helped him the rest of the way through.

"What happened?" she said as he lay dripping and gasping on the floor.

"The barrier must have given way."

He looked over at the trapdoor opening and saw the foaming water lapping at its edges. He pushed himself to his knees as an awful realization hit like a speeding truck.

"Cody . . . he hasn't a chance."

She shook her head. "Don't say that! We've just got to find a phone and—"

A splash and movement in the opening.

Jack rolled away, expecting the creature to emerge. But instead Cody appeared, rising through the churning water as if propelled from behind.

He *was* being propelled. Jack saw a pair of thick, black-furred arms pushing him out of the water. His limp form flopped onto the floor where he rolled over onto his back and lay still.

Jack saw those two furred arms reach over the edge of the doorway, saw the sharp yellow talons of its handlike paws frantically claw at the floor, trying to find purchase, but they couldn't hold. Slowly they slipped toward the opening, leaving gouges in the concrete. Something that could have been a snake or an eel or a smooth tentacle whipped out of the water and waved about as if trying to find something to grip.

And then with a final scrabbling rasp of claws on concrete, the paws slipped through the opening and disappeared along with the eel or whatever it was.

Jack stared in openmouthed shock. It had saved Cody—pushed him out of the water. He kept waiting for the hands to reappear, but they didn't.

He turned to Weezy. "Did you—?"

"Jack!" she cried, pointing to Cody. "He's not breathing!"

Jack leaned over the boy and saw that Weezy was right. His face was white, his lips blue.

Cody Bockman was dead.

16

Maybe not, Jack thought as he sorted through his shell-shocked brain, trying to tease out what he'd learned in life-saving class about drowning victims who weren't breathing.

Pulse—check for pulse!

He thrust two fingertips against Cody's throat, pressing into the flesh about an inch from the midline. He felt a weakly beating artery.

"He's alive!"

"But he's not breathing!" Weezy said. "He needs CPR!"

Right—no!

Can't get air into water-filled lungs, he remembered. Always do a Heimlich first!

Jack lifted Cody's limp body to a sitting position and got behind him. He placed a fist under his breastbone, covered it with another hand and began thrusting.

"What are you *doing*, Jack?" Weezy wailed. "He needs CPR!"

No, he knew he was right.

Suddenly powerful hands tore him away from Cody. He looked up and saw Mr. Drexler's angry face.

"Take over, Eggers," he said to his driver, then looked at Jack and Weezy. "And you . . . you two have caused a big problem."

Jack watched Eggers sling Cody over his shoulder like an empty sack, then begin jouncing the limp little body.

"What's he doing?" Jack said.

"What you were attempting—only better. I assume that's the Bockman boy?"

Jack nodded. "Yes, he—"

"Quickly, Eggers!" Mr. Drexler said. "Take him up to that sinkhole." His expression was stern as he turned to them. "Who do you two think you are, breaking into private property and vandalizing it."

"We didn't vandalize anything!" they replied in unison.

He pointed to the water now bubbling through the opening and spreading over the floor.

"That water is about to irreparably damage a lot of valuable furniture. I call that vandalizing. Shut that trapdoor immediately."

"We can't," Jack said. "The pyramid's down there . . . in the water."

Mr. Drexler looked as if he were about to explode. "You—"

"Who cares about that!" Jack shouted. "Cody's dead!"

He ran for the stairs, pounded up to the first floor and out the open front door. It had stopped raining, but thunder still muttered and grumbled off to the east. Eggers was at the curb, trying Heimlichs on Cody's limp form.

It's no use, Jack thought, feeling his throat lock. He's gone.

And then a sloppy, soggy figure stepped from the shadows.

"Hey, what's goin' down here?" he said.

Jack recognized Walt's voice. He looked like he must have been standing out in the storm the whole time.

"Get away," Eggers said.

"Naw, man," he said, leaning over the boy. His voice sounded clear, not a hint of a slur. "I know this kid. I been waiting for him."

He reached for Cody's hand. Jack noticed with a start that he wasn't wearing gloves.

Waiting for him? Was this why he'd been hanging around Old Town? But how could he possibly—?

He touched Cody's hand and as soon as they made contact, Cody jerked and coughed up what seemed like a quart of water.

Walt staggered back like he'd received a shock, then began to wander away.

"Walt?"

Walt turned and gave him a dazed look, then faded back into the shadows.

When Mrs. Clevenger had told him to stop drinking, she'd said, *You may be needed in the next day or so.* Was this what she'd meant?

What just happened here?

Then Weezy rushed up behind him.

"Jack!" she said as she saw Cody gasping for air in Eggers's arms. "He's alive!" She threw her arms around Jack and squeezed. "He's going to be all right!"

Jack felt his throat tighten. He *was* all right . . . Cody was all right. He might have nightmares the rest of his life, but he was alive.

He felt a surge of pride.

Because of us.

Mr. Drexler appeared. "Well, that will make things less complicated. I called in an emergency. And while we're waiting you two will explain exactly how that child came to be in the Lodge's basement."

Taking turns, Jack and Weezy launched into a rundown of the night's events. Mr. Drexler didn't seem too surprised at anything until they mentioned finding Cody in the lost town.

He held up a hand and stared at them.

"You found him down there? How could he possibly have—?"

"The creature brought him," Jack said.

Mr. Drexler froze as if hit by a paralyzer beam. After a pause he said, "Creature? *What* creature?"

"Some kind of weird bear," Jack said. "We never saw it except for its black furry arms and claws. Oh, and I saw something wormlike stick out of the water at the end."

"I saw it too," Weezy said, glancing at Jack. "Looked like a tentacle but that couldn't be, right?"

Mr. Drexler looked as white as his suit as he leaned heavily on his cane.

"No . . . couldn't be."

"Are you all right?" Weezy said.

Instead of giving an answer he asked a question. "You say this animal brought the child underground. Why would it do that?"

"It was feeding him," Jack said. "Maybe to fatten him up?"

"No," Weezy said. "It was bringing him toys . . . like presents. Maybe it was lonely. It almost seemed to be treating Cody like its own child. Maybe it wanted a child and couldn't have one."

"'Like its own child,'" Mr. Drexler repeated in a soft voice.

Weezy added, "Yes. I mean, it got Cody to safety first, then couldn't save itself. That has to mean something."

Mr. Drexler looked dazed as he shook his head. "Incredible. None of this, however, mitigates your breaking and entering, and the destruction of Lodge property. This will have to be reported to the police."

Jack felt his chest tighten. His folks were going to kill him. Plus he'd have some kind of criminal record.

He glanced at Weezy who looked like he felt.

We're cooked, he thought. Deep fried and well done.

"At least we found Cody," he said. "So it wasn't all for nothing." He looked at Mr. Drexler. "Do you have to report us?"

The man gave him a disgusted look, then his features relaxed. "Perhaps something can be worked out."

"What?" Weezy said, straightening. "Anything."

Jack's mood lightened at the ray of hope, but he was wary of this man.

"I wish to exclude all mention of the Lodge or the Order from this," Mr. Drexler said. "Even though it hasn't been opened in perhaps a century, I do not wish it known that the building's basement housed a trapdoor into the underground."

Jack said, "But Cody will—"

"The child was unconscious during his brief time in the basement. He nearly drowned in the underground and came to up here on the street. He will have no idea he was ever in the Lodge. But the same cannot be said of you two."

"You want us to say we were never in there?" Weezy said. "But he saw us underground. He'll remember that."

"Of course he will."

Jack raised his hands. This didn't make any sense. "Then how do we explain how we got underground?"

Mr. Drexler stopped and pointed to the front yard of the house next door.

"You'll say you fell through there."

Jack looked and didn't see what he was talking about.

Suddenly Cody struggled to his feet and stumbled toward them.

Crying, "Cody!" Weezy ran to him and he fell into her arms. "Jack!" she said, lifting the boy. "Look!"

And then he saw it: a six-foot-wide hole in the front lawn—the sinkhole Mr. Drexler had mentioned.

"I noticed the lake was lower on the way in," Mr. Drexler said. "And when I saw that sink hole, I instantly realized what was happening. But I had no idea . . ." His words drifted off as he stared in Cody's direction.

"Why did you come back?"

"Hmm?" His attention returned from wherever it had been. "I didn't at first. We'd stopped for a bite to eat when I realized we'd left something behind."

"The pyramid."

"No." He gave Jack a look. "That belongs here. Now I suppose it's lost forever, thanks to you and your girlfriend."

Jack wasn't going to let that pass. "Just as lost as it would still be if we hadn't found it in the Pines."

Mr. Drexler stared at him, and Jack stared right back.

"And she's not my girlfriend," he added.

After a moment Mr. Drexler said, "Be that as it may, I sent Eggers back and he found the door unlocked. When he returned to me and reported that the pyramid was missing, I knew exactly who was to blame. But I wanted to see for myself before visiting your and the Connell girl's parents. Upon my return I noticed the basement lights on. You know the rest."

Jack jumped at a loud crunching, sucking sound to his right. He looked and saw a section of the street's asphalt caving in not thirty feet away.

Another sinkhole.

"You can expect many more of those in Old Town before the night is over. The lost town is crumbling beneath us."

"Will there be anything left of it?"

"I doubt it."

Jack pointed to the original hole. "So . . . we say we fell in there and found Cody. How did we get out?"

"The flood waters floated you high enough to climb out. The revised story is essentially true. All you are changing is the location of your ingress and egress. In exchange, I do not press charges." He gave a small, condescending smile. "That way the two of you can become big heroes in your little world."

Jack didn't want to be a hero, and was already working on ways to play down his role, reducing it to just happening to be in the right place at the right time. The real hero—at the end, at least—was the animal. It had died saving Cody. Of course, Cody wouldn't have needed saving if it had left him alone in the first place.

The animal . . . Jack had a feeling Mr. Drexler knew something about it.

"What do we say about the animal down there?"

Mr. Drexler fixed his gaze a thousand miles away. "Say whatever you wish."

"Not much to say since none of us saw it."

"Then perhaps the less said, the better. The child's story will be confused and garbled, and will change again and again. No sense in causing undue alarm over a creature that is undoubtedly dead."

"What was it?"

Mr. Drexler kept his gaze averted. "I have no idea."

"Yes, you do. You reacted when we told you about it."

Finally he looked at Jack. "I assure you I do not know

what it was. I have an idea what it might have been, but . . ."

"But?"

"What it might have been should have died a long, long time ago. It seems impossible that it could have survived this long."

Frustration flooded Jack. Mr. Drexler was answering the question without telling him anything.

"But what 'might' it have been?"

"Let's just call it a bear . . . an unusual breed of bear."

Whatever Jack had seen of the creature could be considered bearish . . . except maybe for that tentacle thing. Okay . . . a mutant bear or some such.

"Could it or one of its ancestors have been caged in that stone pyramid out by the mound?"

Mr. Drexler stared at him for a long moment. "You do get around, don't you."

The wail of a siren filtered through the night. Jack looked down Quakerton Road and saw flashing red lights heading their way.

"Do we have a deal?" Mr. Drexler said.

Jack nodded. "Deal. I'll fill Weezy in. And I guess I'm fired, right?"

The dark eyebrows lifted. "Fired? Why would I fire you?"

"Well, I thought—"

"Oh, no. I want you where I can keep an eye on you."

1

"I should have stayed with you guys!" Eddie said for what had to be the thousandth time as they walked toward the bus stop. He was toying with his Rubik's Cube, absently twisting it back and forth without looking at it. "Why didn't I *stay*?"

"'Cause you're a wimp," Jack told him.

"I am! I am! Wimpacious maximus!"

They'd told him pretty much the same story they'd told everyone else, but with a special variation since Eddie knew they'd been in the Lodge. They told him they hadn't found the pyramid and had fallen into the sinkhole after leaving the building.

"I could be a hero now like you guys!"

"Not until you straighten out that cube—or let a genius like me do it for you."

"And let you be a Rubik's hero too? As if."

"We're not heroes," Weezy said. "Please stop saying that."

"But you are! Man, if I'd been with you guys when you found Cody, I'd be wearing a Superman cape to school today."

"Then I'm glad you weren't," she said, glancing at Jack.

Yeah. Jack was glad too. There'd be no way of keeping a lid on Eddie. Sooner or later he'd spill the beans about being in the Lodge, ruining their deal with Mr. Drexler.

Jack and Weezy had quickly discussed it last night during

the turmoil of the ambulance's arrival. Neither wanted the attention that was coming, so they agreed to minimize their role in Cody's rescue.

When they were questioned—by Tim, who'd shown up even though it wasn't his shift—they told him they'd fallen through the sinkhole, heard Cody's cries, and climbed back out with him.

What of Cody's story of a monster keeping him prisoner?

We don't know . . . we never saw it. Too dark to see anything down there.

What you did was very brave. You're heroes.

We're not. We literally fell into the situation and did what anyone else would have done.

And that was the way it had gone. Jack asked Tim to keep their names out of it as much as possible. He'd seemed puzzled by the request but said he'd do what he could.

"How's your head?" Weezy asked.

He touched the tender area of scalp at the rear, gooey now with Neosporin.

"Okay, I guess."

The EMTs had looked at it last night and told him he'd be better off with stitches but, because it wasn't a full-thickness cut, didn't absolutely need them. Jack had opted for a little first-aid treatment.

His mother had almost fainted when she saw the blood on his shirt, but recovered and was suitably proud when Tim told her and Dad about Jack finding Cody.

He still didn't understand what it had been about his blood that turned the animal off. Not that he was unhappy about that—no way. Just curious.

Curious about Walt too. Had it been pure coincidence that Cody had come to when Walt touched him, or . . .

Or what?

You may be needed in the next day or so . . .

This was all so crazy.

His folks had given him the option of staying home today, but he wanted to go in. Word of the rescue would be spreading through school and he wanted to be there to douse any hero talk. Being a hero meant attention. Neither he nor Weezy wanted that. He wasn't sure of Weezy's reasons, but he knew she was self-conscious and probably figured the more people looked at her, the more flaws they'd find. He just wanted to be Jack . . . just Jack . . . a kid who could walk the halls and go where he wanted when he wanted without anyone paying much attention.

Yeah. No hero stuff. At least not on the outside. But inside he was feeling pretty damn good. He'd put Mr. Vivino in his place and found a lost child almost given up for dead.

Not bad for a night's work.

Except for one thing . . .

"Think we'll ever see that little pyramid again?"

Weezy closed her eyes and flinched—as if the question had caused physical pain.

He knew the answer, but wondered if Weezy could accept it. He had a wild vision of her at the controls of a backhoe digging up the streets of Old Town in search of the buried city and her pyramid.

"I don't want to talk about it."

"Well, then—"

"Okay, yes, I do. It's gone for good, buried under Old Town. I know that. It makes me want to scream when I think of it lost down there, but it's better than knowing it's sitting on a shelf in the Lodge. I want it back like crazy, but I have to accept that it's gone. At least it wasn't stolen from us this time . . . we lost it. There's a big difference—at least to me—if that makes any sense."

"It does, kind of." He looked at her. "You mean that?"

"Yeah . . . for the moment, anyway. I may feel entirely different by the time we get to school, but right now I see it as sort of a circle: The buried pyramid was uncovered—because of us. And now it's buried again—because of us. Don't you feel like a circle has closed?"

A circle closed . . . Had Weezy too noticed how recent events in their lives seemed to circle the pyramid?

"Yeah, I do. I definitely do."

Jack felt a surge of relief, followed by a strange peace as they reached the highway.

He figured all the Johnson kids had heard—the word would have spread like the flu through the close-knit community—but the only out-of-town kids who'd know would be those who listened to the morning news on the local radio.

When they reached the highway he glanced right and was surprised to see Mrs. Vivino waiting at the elementary bus stop. Sally stood to the side with a couple of little kids while a group of the other mothers clustered close around her mother. No way they hadn't heard.

The events at the VFW seemed like they'd happened weeks ago rather than just last night.

To his shock, Mrs. V broke away from the other women and began walking toward him.

"Jack? Can I speak to you?"

Jack stood frozen. What could she have to say to him?

Something about her expression made him want to say "No" and cross the street. But he hung tough.

"You two go ahead," he said to Weezy and Eddie, as he walked toward Mrs. V.

"I suppose you heard about the videotape," she said as they drew within a few feet of each other.

Jack nodded, his mouth dry. "Um, yeah. Sorry."

"I'm glad you found Cody. I'm glad for him, and I'm glad for his parents, and I'm glad because it gives people something to talk about besides that tape."

"Yeah, well . . ."

He wanted to say more but felt tongue-tied.

"Do you know who made it?"

Oh jeez. He could feel every muscle in his body tensing. Why was she asking him? She couldn't suspect, could she? No reason in the world she could. He forced himself to look at her and saw a distorted image of himself reflected in her sunglasses.

"I haven't heard any rumors or anything."

"I'm sure that person thought he was doing us a favor, but he invaded our privacy. He stole what was supposed to be just between two people, and made it public."

Stole? *Stole*?

"People see one thing, one scene from a marriage and don't understand. They don't know what went before. They don't know what someone was like before . . . before he lost his son . . . how when a parent's worst nightmare becomes a reality, how that can change a person . . . make him into someone he never was, someone he would never have wanted to be."

Was she excusing all that violence?

She said, "That videotape changed everything. A family splits, a home will have to be sold, Sally will have to move away from her friends."

A tear slipped from under her sunglasses and left a glistening trail down her cheek. She wiped it away.

"Everybody loses . . . except maybe the videotaper, who probably thinks he's some sort of hero. If you ever meet him, tell him he's not. Tell him he may have had good intentions, but the road to Hell is paved with those."

Jack watched in stunned silence as she turned and walked back toward Sally.

She knew. Somehow . . . she knew.

He wanted to go after her and defend himself, wanted to say that if she was going to let that go on in her house just to keep her marriage together at any cost, fine for her. But what about the cost to Sally? Sally wasn't being given a choice. Sally had stopped smiling.

But he couldn't say a word without giving himself away.

Maybe Mr. Vivino had been changed by Tony's death, or maybe he'd just stopped controlling an awful temper. Jack could only judge the man by his actions, by what he *did*, and what he'd been doing was wrong.

But what about what I did? he thought.

He'd intruded on a private matter. Was peeping into their life and videotaping it right?

He'd thought so at the time. Now he wasn't so sure.

But if you saw something wrong, was it ever right to turn away and just mind your own damn business?

On the other hand, had exposure robbed them of the chance of working things out?

Jack shook his whirling head. What had seemed so clearly black and white a few days ago had blurred to gray in the middle. If he could go back in time a week, he wondered, would he do the same thing?

Yeah, he decided, hearing again the *smack* against Sally's wet suit, seeing her knocked down. Yeah, he probably would. It would still seem like the right thing to do. But he knew now that doing the right thing didn't guarantee a rosy outcome. Or a warm fuzzy feeling.

He caught Sally staring at him. He forced a smile and managed to give her a little wave. She waved back.

But she didn't smile.

2

"Hi, Jack."

He'd been following Weezy and Eddie onto the bus, lost in thought and feeling glum. He looked and saw Karina, with her engineer's cap, baggy sweater, and jeans, smiling up at him from a window seat. The aisle seat next to her was empty.

"Oh, hi."

"Need a seat?" she said, her eyes inviting.

He looked around. "Where's Cristin?"

"Not feeling so hot."

He spotted Eddie slipping into an empty seat and Weezy heading for her sophomore friends toward the rear. So he stowed his backpack under the seat and dropped in next to Karina.

"I heard they found Cody last night," she said.

Swell. She listened to the morning news. Then he realized that if anyone on this bus listened, it would be Karina.

"Yeah. Great news."

"What happened? Who found him?"

Okay, play it cool.

"Couple of local kids."

He hid a smile, wondering at her reaction when she discovered she'd been sitting next to one of those kids and he hadn't told her. She'd probably think that was pretty cool.

He found he liked the idea of Karina thinking him cool.

He felt a tap on his shoulder and looked up to see Eddie holding out his Rubik's.

"Okay, boy genius. I give up. You've been talking big. Let's see you deliver."

Jack took it and turned it over this way and that, saying, "Boy, you really messed it up."

"Yeah. It's a gift. I did my part, now you do yours."

"I'll have it back to you by the time we get to school."

Eddie laughed. "Yeah, right."

Jack looked up at him. "You doubt my Rubik-fu?"

"Hey, if you can straighten that out by school, I'll carry you from class to class on my back."

"Deal."

The driver gave Eddie her no-standing-in-the-aisle line, so he returned to his seat.

Karina stared at the cube. "Can you really straighten that out by school?"

He smiled. "Of course not."

"Then why . . . ?"

He pulled his backpack from beneath the seat, unzipped it, and removed a new, unused Rubik's Cube.

"I've been setting him up for this all week."

Karina slapped a hand over her mouth to stifle a laugh. "You are eeeeevil!"

"A regular devil in disguise," he said as he hid the old cube in his backpack.

"Oh that's so funny! He's going to totally plotz when he sees it." She laughed again. "First Cody, now this. Almost makes up for that awfulness at the VFW last night."

Jack nearly jumped out of his seat. "How'd you hear about that?"

"My dad's a vet. He was there. I heard him telling my mother."

Jack realized he'd never met Karina's father, so he couldn't have known.

"How do you feel about that?"

She shrugged. "Serves him right."

Her lack of hesitation surprised Jack. Then he remembered Mrs. V's words and decided to bounce them off Karina.

"But . . . someone invaded their privacy."

"Yeah, true, but he was running for public office. Don't people have a right to know who they're voting for? I want to know *everything* about anybody who's going to be making decisions that affect me."

"Everyone's got a right to privacy."

She nodded. "Absolutely. But if you want privacy, don't go public. A man with a secret life shouldn't step into the spotlight and expect to keep his secrets."

Jack had a secret life—things he couldn't talk about to anyone. He vowed then never to run for any sort of public office.

But didn't everyone have a secret life? Even the animal in the buried town had had a secret life.

"I think it comes down to truth," she added. "Isn't the truth important?"

"Very."

She raised a fist. "Truth."

"But what *is* truth?" he asked, just to see how she'd react.

"The truth is."

He waited. She said no more, simply watched him, smiling.

"That's it?"

She nodded. "Yep. The truth is. We can twist it every which way with our minds and our words, but that doesn't change the truth. The truth is what trips you up when you walk around with your eyes closed."

I like you, Karina Haddon, Jack thought.

"You're a thinker, aren't you."

She frowned. "Been told I think too much."

He nudged her. "Well, someone's got to make up for all the people who don't think at all."

She leaned against him as she laughed. He liked the feeling and liked the sound. "Thank you! I'll use that next time I'm accused of thinking too much."

"Who tells you that?"

Her smile faded. "My father, mostly."

That rang a familiar bell.

"Wants you to be a bow-head?"

Her jaw dropped. "How do you *know*?"

"I know someone with the same problem."

"Really? How does she deal with it?"

He glanced back at Weezy, reading a book.

"She stays herself."

"Not easy sometimes."

He nudged her. "Stay you. You're great just the way you are."

Instantly sure he'd said too much, he wanted to recall those last words. But then he saw Karina give a secret little fist pump and knew it was okay.

They sat in silence a moment and Jack thought about what Weezy had said.

Don't you feel that a circle has closed?

Yeah. More than one.

He thought about how complicated his life had become—a series of intersecting circles all leading back to that strange little pyramid.

Was it good or evil, or like what they'd been learning about in chemistry: a catalyst . . . something that kicked off reactions?

One circle had led to the deaths of a number of Lodge members—one of them a freeholder—but had exposed Steve Brussard's problems. If Steve was getting help, that was a good thing.

But the death of that freeholder had led Mr. Vivino to run for his spot, and accidentally brought Jack back into the circle of Tony's family. Jack had thought that had resolved to a good end until talking to Mrs. V this morning. Now he wasn't so sure.

Another pyramid circle had led them to the Lodge last night. Because of that, Cody Bockman was alive and with his folks this morning. He'd have drowned if Jack and Weezy hadn't gone looking for the pyramid.

Circles within circles . . . wheels within wheels . . . gears in the machinery of his life, turning and turning.

Was that what the pyramid was—a catalyst?

If so, maybe losing it was a good thing.

Or maybe not.

The last couple of months had been pretty interesting.

May you live in interesting times . . . wasn't that an old Chinese curse?

But Karina . . . none of the circles involved her. She was outside the pyramid zone. And that seemed a good thing.

He liked being with her. She was like Weezy in some ways—smart, opinionated, a thinker—but different in others. He liked her slant on things.

May you live in interesting times . . .

Jack sensed he had more interesting times ahead. He just hoped they weren't *too* interesting.

<www.repairmanjack.com>

AUTHOR'S NOTE

For readers who wish to know a little more about Weird Walt and the secret behind his odd behavior, I suggest the recent reprint of *The Touch*. The novel's prequel, "Dat Tay Vao," is included. Together they offer a glimpse into the gift/curse that rules Walter Erskine's life.

A reader's guide for *Jack: Secret Circles* is available online at http://tor-forge.com/jacksecretcircles.

THE SECRET HISTORY OF THE WORLD

The preponderance of my work deals with a history of the world that remains undiscovered, unexplored, and unknown to most of humanity. Some of this secret history has been revealed in the Adversary Cycle, some in the Repairman Jack novels, and bits and pieces in other, seemingly unconnected works. Taken together, even these millions of words barely scratch the surface of what has been going on behind the scenes, hidden from the workaday world. I've listed these works below in the chronological order in which the events in them occur.

Note: "Year Zero" is the end of civilization as we know it; "Year Zero Minus One" is the year preceding it, etc.

THE PAST

"Demonsong" (prehistory)
"Aryans and Absinthe"** (1923–1924)
Black Wind (1926–1945)
The Keep (1941)
Reborn (February–March 1968)
"Dat Tay Vao"*** (March 1968)
Jack: Secret Histories (1983)
Jack: Secret Circles (1983)

YEAR ZERO MINUS THREE

"Faces"* (early summer)
The Tomb (summer)

"The Barrens"* (ends in September)
"A Day in the Life"* (October)
"The Long Way Home"
Legacies (December)

YEAR ZERO MINUS TWO

Conspiracies (April) (includes "Home Repairs")
"Interlude at Duane's"** (April)
All the Rage (May) (includes "The Last Rakosh")
Hosts (June)
The Haunted Air (August)
Gateways (September)
Crisscross (November)
Infernal (December)

YEAR ZERO MINUS ONE

Harbingers (January)
Bloodline (April)
By the Sword (May)
Ground Zero (July)
The Touch (ends in August)
The Peabody-Ozymandias Traveling Circus & Oddity Emporium (ends in September)
"Tenants"*

YEAR ZERO

"Pelts"*
Reprisal (ends in February)
Repairman Jack #14 (February)
the last Repairman Jack novel (April)
Nightworld (starts in May)

Reprisal will be back in print before too long. I'm planning a total of fifteen Repairman Jack novels (not counting the young adult titles), ending the Secret History with the publication of a heavily revised *Nightworld.*

*available in *The Barrens and Others*

**available in *Aftershock & Others*

***available in the 2009 reissue of *The Touch*